A VIOLENT SHOCK
RAN THROUGH HER . . .

When she saw him arrive, she felt her nerves jerk as though in contact with fire. But she came forward smilingly, as though he were just another guest.

The guests in the background fell silent, watching with close attention this meeting between the deposed heir and his usurping enemy.

There was cool derision in Falcon's blue eyes as he took the hand she held out and lifted it to his lips. His eyes remained fixed on her face, and as his mouth touched her fingers, he saw her wince, heard a tiny intake of breath and felt her quiver.

He straightened, looking down into her face with that old, intimate, secret smile. "You are a constant amazement to me. I had supposed it impossible for you to increase in beauty, yet you have managed it." His tone was lazy, warm, as though nothing of what had happened had even been.

While she was still stricken dumb with confused anger, Falcon looked past her at his cousin, his brows lifted quizzically, the derisive smile lingering on his mouth.

"My dear Roger," he drawled, "I must congratulate you on your wife. She is even more enchanting than when I last saw her." His own jealousy and hurt made the words dagger-sharp.

Roger's lips drew back from his teeth in a snarl. Sabine's heart leapt into her mouth. This was what she had feared. Falcon had come determined to cause trouble.

MAIDEN CASTLE

Sheila Holland

PLAYBOY PRESS
PAPERBACKS

CHAPTER ONE

ONE windy spring morning some five years after the battle of Waterloo, a girl could have been seen walking up the green slopes of Maiden Castle, in Dorset, a rush basket over her arm, the brown folds of her cloak continually blowing back behind her, giving the appearance of wings when seen from a distance. She was of middle height, slim, and walked with a brisk yet graceful step, keeping her head bent down slightly in order to keep her wide-brimmed straw bonnet from blowing away.

She reached the final crest and stood there, staring back the way she had come, over rising and falling green embankments against which the white chalk showed, where grazing sheep had bitten the grass down to the very roots.

Moisture stood in her eyes, not brought there by the wind which rushed with such a violence over the ancient fortifications, but by the realization, which she felt deeply, that she was leaving her home forever.

It was a lonely place in which she found herself, rising up out of the valley like a great green wave, empty of everything human, inhabited only by sheep and the larks which she could hear singing all around her. She knew nothing of the history

of Maiden Castle apart from the word-of-mouth
legends passed on by country people for centuries,
but had she been a total stranger to it, it would
somehow have conveyed its own myth in the very
emptiness of its grassy bowls and steep sides. A
presence seemed to lurk there invisibly, and she
glanced around half-nervously as if expecting to
be surprised at any moment.

The place suited her mood perfectly, but then
the wind-driven clouds blew apart, and the sun
shone through, bathing the hills in golden light.

Her mood lifted. She ran down the slope,
climbed a stile and came into a narrow track
strewn with flints and stones which ran between
two high embankments.

From the head of this small valley, she could
see the roofs of Dorchester glinting in the morning
sunlight, and her heart thudded in anticipation.

She was walking into the county town to meet
her new employer and had walked the five miles
from her village, Twyne Abbas, since leaving
home at seven o'clock. Looking up at the sky
again, she judged the hour to stand nearly at eight.
She had time in hand and was hungry since she
had left the house without breakfast in her haste
to be on time.

Looking about, she chose a small hollow in the
bank and flung herself down on the grass. Her
appearance had startled some bland-faced ewes
grazing nearby, and they skipped off, their belled
necks chiming, out of sight behind the bank.

Unpacking some bread and cheese from her
basket, she leaned back, nibbling slowly, staring

around. The clouds were moving away fast. Bright patches of blue unrolled overhead, promising a fine day. It was warm in the hollow out of the wind, and the heat of the sun began to bring out almost invisible coils of steamy mist from the damp earth.

As she ate, she pushed back her straw bonnet, revealing thick, honey-colored hair worn very plainly dressed. Her wide eyes were of that strange opalescent color, something between green and blue, which changes with the light or the mood. They were set beneath faint brows, giving added height to her forehead. Her generously curved mouth seemed to smile, even in repose, and had small laughter lines set around its corners. The dimples in her cheeks underlined the general sweetness of her expression so that strangers would smile at her in the street as she passed and turn their heads to look after her with a feeling of loss.

She was the eldest daughter of a shepherd, Daniel Mudeford, who bore a continual grudge against the world and fate for having failed to live up to his expectations. The only son of a wealthy farmer, he had been educated to expect more of life than life had been prepared to offer, and when his father was ruined by a succession of wrong decisions and bad harvests, Daniel had been forced to work on another man's farm. To set his daughter apart from other children, he had given her the name Sabine, dimly remembered from his school days as one with glamorous associations, and had stubbornly resisted the vicar when he attempted to dissuade him.

" 'Tis not a Christian name," the other villagers had said, shaking their heads in disapproval.

The three children who followed Sabine into the world did not live to be christened at all, which confirmed Daniel Mudeford in his belief that he was persecuted by fate.

Her mother, Lucy, was crushed by the deaths of her other three children. A large, silent, submissive woman with the blank brown eyes of a milch cow and a heavy walk, she died when Sabine was ten years old.

"I shall not marry again," her father said after the funeral. "I shall not tempt fate so far." His resentment had passed through a stage of anger into one of gloomy satisfaction, as though his wife's death had set the seal on his belief in his own ill luck, and had given him a feeling of being different from other men, a being set apart from the common run.

Sabine was not sorry to leave his cottage when the chance arose. His clouded mind overshadowed hers.

Master Bourne of Twyneham Farm married late in life, and Sabine's cheerful good looks attracted the attention of the new bride. The girl was offered the post of personal maid, and she eagerly accepted.

For four years, her life passed very pleasantly. She was quick to learn and a lively companion, so that her mistress grew very fond of her. But then the farm was darkened by the death of

Mistress Bourne in childbed, and Sabine had to leave Twynehams. The stricken farmer shut himself up alone to drink himself blind to his grief, and when Sabine returned to her father's cottage, it was to find him preparing to leave it himself.

He had accepted a post as shepherd on a farm in Yorkshire and was leaving within a month.

"You must go to t'Hiring Fair at Dorchester," he advised her. "You'll surely get a place there."

But the parson, when his advice was sought, had a better idea. "I know of a young lady looking for someone to serve her as a maid," he told her. "It would be a great improvement for you, my dear. You can read, can you not? And sew neatly?"

"Yes, sir," she agreed. "Mistress Bourne taught me to read and write. And I can do plain sewing."

"Then I think I can recommend you for this post," he nodded. "The Squire of Ceorlbury has a sister, Miss Amhurst, who has lately come home from London and is in need of a personal maid. Leave the matter with me, Sabine, and I will write to her for you."

Two weeks later, he had sent for her and told her that she was engaged, on approval, and must make her way to Dorchester where she would be met by someone from Ceorlbury.

"Is it a big house, sir?" she asked eagerly.

He looked surprised. "Have you never heard of it?"

She shook her head. "Why, no, I cannot say I ever did."

"Well, it is a great estate, some miles from

Dorchester, with three or four farms and a grand park which is well stocked with deer and pheasants. My cousin is vicar there, which is how I know the family so well. Miss Amhurst was not pleased with any of the local girls. It is so long since a woman lived at Ceorlbury that their manners are a little rough, I gather."

"Mercy," breathed Sabine, awed by the thought of living in so grand a place.

"Now, you must not be nervous. Mistress Bourne has trained you well." He sighed. The late mistress of Twyneham Farm had married beneath her, for love, and had brought to the district a new gentleness which he had hoped would continue for many years. The vicar had been very slightly in love with Mistress Bourne, and her death had saddened him.

And so that morning Sabine had set out in her best brown gown, wearing a clean white handkerchief crossed over her throat, her cloak loosely hanging from her shoulders, to walk across the fields to Dorchester.

She was young enough to be excited by this change in her life, inexperienced enough to be nervous, and influenced by her father's pessimism into a reaction of optimism. It seemed to her that she began life again on a bright morning with the whole world spread out before her.

Above her the larks hung like black moths on invisible strings, singing their hearts out before, with an effortless swoop, they skated down the wind and disappeared behind the embankments.

Their song seemed full of promise, vibrant with happiness.

She stood up, shook her gown clear of crumbs, tied her cloak closer round her throat, resettled her bonnet and tied its brown ribbons at the side of her chin. Then she resumed her walk along the path which ran through the fields into Dorchester.

She had rarely been here before and was fascinated by everything she saw. The town was in the middle of the upheaval always accompanying market day. The narrow streets were crowded with men and women carrying baskets, or driving geese or sheep, noisily greeting each other in passing when they met a long-unseen acquaintance. Through this turmoil Sabine passed unnoticed and made her way to the Spanish Sailor Inn near a narrow bridge over the river.

Over the door swung a sign showing a darkvisaged man with gold earrings, behind whose shoulders was painted a galleon in full sail.

"Jabez Starling?" repeated the landlord, rubbing his hands upon his stained apron, "Aye, he is here." And led her to a small parlor where at a table sat a slight, gray-haired man with stooped shoulders and a thoughtful expression who looked round as she entered and stared at her.

"The young woman you was expecting, Jabez," the landlord said, and withdrew.

"Come here, girl," the other man said quietly.

She obeyed, curtseying as she stood at his side. He looked her over with a raised eyebrow.

"Seems Parson was right," he said. "I think you'll please our Miss Bella right enough." Then he stood up and walked towards the door. "I have business here in Dorchester so you shall have to wait for me until noon. Have ye money enough?"

She could not imagine what she would need money for, but drew out a handful of pennies to show him silently.

He nodded. "Good. Then I'll see ye at noon here. Ye had best eat your dinner here before we set out. I shall eat elsewhere." And he was gone before she could reply.

She went out again and wandered around the busy town, staring at the shops and market stalls, watching the farmers bargaining for sheep, feeling the waves of people beat around her with stupefied passivity. Gradually the noise began to make her head ache, and she longed for the silence of Maiden Castle again and the sweet song of the larks.

Then she went back to the Spanish Sailor and ate a simple dinner of stewed mutton and cabbage before rejoining Jabez Starling.

"Come along," he said. "I'm wishful to get a good start before the roads are crowded. Are ye ready?"

Clutching her basket, she nodded and followed him into the inn yard where she was ordered to mount up behind him on a fat, stolid cob the color of chestnuts in autumn.

She looked back as they left the town behind, wondering when she would see it again, and thought of her father, even then making his way up north on a wagon.

A little sob caught in her throat, and she stiffened to resist it.

"Sit still, girl," muttered Jabez over his shoulder. "You're jogging up and down like a sack of oats. You'll be saddle sore before we get home."

Later, he burst into song, and when he turned his head to speak to her again, she realized that he had been drinking during the morning. His breath was stale with hops, and his face flushed.

"You're a lucky girl," he told her seriously. "Miss Bella would have none of our village girls. She is too nice in her ways since she came home from London." He laughed. "Ah, but she is single still, for all the gold squire spent to get rid of her."

Sabine was baffled by this remark. Why should the squire spend money to be rid of his sister?

But she did not dare to question Jabez Starling, and he went on to explain that he was the bailiff on the Ceorlbury estate. "The Amhursts are all powerful set against marriage," he said sleepily. "Slow begetters and slow to change their minds," he told her, before lapsing into silence again, his head sunk down upon his chest.

The cob trotted on without his guidance, apparently knowing the road back to its stable too well to need direction, and soon they came within sight of a high, red-brick wall.

The cob broke into a faster trot, and Jabez woke and bawled, "Whoa, whoa, ye damned limb of Satan . . ."

Over his shoulder he told Sabine, "That is Ceorlbury."

The wall ran on for what seemed miles, rising and falling alongside the road. She could see the tops of elms above it, black with rooks' nests, and when they turned in at a pair of wrought-iron gates in whose centers was a shield bearing a confused set of devices, she found herself staring across a great park.

"That is the Amhurst arms," Jabez explained, pointing to the gates. "A mailed fist holding a dagger, a great bird, and a leopard. I can't say what they mean. Even Squire don't rightly know. They have been in the family countless years, though."

She was too awed by the park to heed him. It rolled away downhill to a narrow stream, its green slopes dotted with oaks and elms, and beyond the stream a lawn rose to a great black and white timbered house, built with two wings, in the shape of an E, the leaded windows gleaming in the afternoon light.

She had never seen anything so beautiful.

The cob trotted on briskly under an avenue of lime trees that lined the road, crossed a narrow bridge over the stream, turned to the right and passed behind the house into a stable yard.

A groom was crouched beside a tall roan mare, examining her legs. He looked round and stood up, grinning at Sabine.

"Where did she spring from?" he asked Jabez, who gruffly told him to mind his own business and get on with his work.

As he led her into the house, he said softly, "This is a house overrun with men, my dear. You must take care not to encourage them. They have bold, rough ways with a maid."

They went by a narrow passage and up a long flight of winding stairs to a landing lit only by the light which fell from a small window high up on the wall.

Jabez threw open a door nearby and ushered Sabine into a little room. "Your new maid, Miss Bella," he said, standing back so that Sabine might pass.

She halted in the center of the room, looking at its only occupant.

She was a tall, thin young woman with black hair, which hung in unbecoming ringlets around her angular face. Her gown was a dark blue check material, gathered at the bodice, brought in by a dark belt, and falling with fullness to her feet.

She was sitting at a table with a book open in her hand and gave Sabine as much study as the girl was giving her new mistress.

"You did not knock, Jabez," was all she said, however, in a severe tone.

He scratched his head, as though baffled, and said, "Well, now, I'm sorry for that. I forgot, d'ye see."

"Do not forget again. Your old, loose ways will not do now that I am home again."

"No, Miss Bella," he said a little suddenly and withdrew.

The young woman now turned her attention to

Sabine with a faint smile. "Mr. Pine told me that you can read and write," she said.

"Yes, ma'am," Sabine whispered.

"You went to your village school, I suppose?"

"No, ma'am, my late mistress taught me."

Bella Amhurst looked up. "Oh, yes, I remember. She died recently, I gather."

"In childbed," Sabine said sadly.

The other woman's face darkened. She closed her book with a petulant slap and stood up. "I hope you understand your duties, girl. You will wait on me each morning before I get up, bring me hot water, lay out my clothes and help me to dress." She picked up a sweetmeat from a bowl which lay nearby and bit into it, then went on talking for some time of what she expected Sabine to do each day.

Bella Amhurst was not an attractive woman. She was just past thirty, awkward of movement, sharp of voice and manner, and prone to fits of hysteria when her will was crossed. This temper had left its mark upon her face, which had temper lines running from nose to mouth.

She had a great deal of excess energy that she unloosed upon the household for want of any other object, bending her mind to the reorganization of the daily routine of the servants with such acidity that some of them threatened to run off and find places elsewhere.

Sabine was kept busy sewing new underwear and linen for her mistress whenever her presence was not required to wait upon Bella. When, however, Bella sat in her private parlor, she had

Sabine sit with her in lieu of better company, and, discovering that the girl had a sweet voice, delighted in having her sing while Bella clumsily sketched views of the park from her window.

Sabine met the squire on the day after her arrival. He came into the parlor, halted and stared at the other girl.

"The new maid?" he asked his sister.

"Yes," said Bella indifferently. "What do you want, Roger?"

He ignored her, putting a finger under Sabine's chin to lift her flushed face. She looked up, seeing a man of about forty, broad in the shoulder, taller than his sister, his head massive and arrogant under thick, black hair. He wore his clothes in casual disarray. They were old and shabby with wear. His nose was large and hooked, his face heavy, his mouth very wide.

"What's your name, girl?" he asked, returning her gaze with equal curiosity.

"Sabine, sir."

His brows rose, thick and black. "Where did you get such a name, for God's sake?"

"My father, sir," she said in embarrassment.

"What was he, by the lord Harry? Some hedge-parson, eh?"

"He was a shepherd, sir, but he had some learning."

Her tone held a trace of resentment at his amusement, and the squire grinned at her.

"Well, he did rightly in giving you that name, my little Sabine shepherdess. You would tempt the sternest Roman from his righteous path."

Bella Amhurst stiffened beside Sabine. "Run along, now, girl," she said quickly, and Sabine eagerly obeyed.

Roger Amhurst looked at his sister, one brow crooked. "I have no designs upon your little serving maid," he said dryly. "I was but teasing her."

"You have all forgotten how to behave here at Ceorlbury," said Bella primly. "I was amazed to find such laxity among the servants. When Amelia was alive, you would not have permitted the slackness and idleness which has reigned here since her death."

He frowned angrily. "This is my house, Bella. Remember that. I do not object if you amuse yourself by governing the servants, but do not try to govern me." And he stalked out, slamming the door behind him.

His sister stood staring at the door, a sigh escaping her. She wondered why her brother had never remarried. He had been married for fifteen years to a rather dull, conventional woman who had not borne him children and had bored him into long hours of work about his estate. Bella had expected him to put someone else in Amelia's place so soon as was decently convenient, but he remained a widower and showed no sign of wishing to marry again.

Bella Amhurst was not suited for a country life, and soon grew restless and eager for new faces. Her brother, she decided, should be coaxed into remarrying, and since there were no suitable brides at hand, she decided to persuade him to invite some young people down from London. The

nearest male relative eligible to inherit Ceorlbury
was their cousin, Falcon Amhurst, whose father
had been Roger's uncle, and whose mother had
brought a fortune into the family by inheriting
from her father, founder of a famous city firm of
merchants.

"No," declared Roger, when she suggested the
visit. "The boy would bring down a parcel of
jabbering idiots and expect me to let them loose
over my land with a gun. Men that hardly know
one end of a gun from the other. As likely to
shoot a gamekeeper as a pheasant! Damn it, no—
I'll not disrupt my quiet life for you."

"It is your duty," she insisted, reddening dan-
gerously. "Falcon is your heir. He should visit
here."

"I'm not senile, yet," he retorted, glowering. "I
may marry again."

"I see no signs of it," she said. "And Falcon is
a very attractive man now. He is popular in
London society."

"Popinjay!" snorted Roger. "Why must you be
so busy always?"

"I am only trying to show you your duty," she
snapped.

"I know my duty well enough, thank you," he
said, and slammed out of the room before she
could continue the discussion.

Sabine was sorry for him, badgered into fury
by his sister, but she could not help hoping that
he would give in and allow the visit.

Bella Amhurst talked endlessly to her of her
fine London friends, and Sabine was on fire

to see them all. She had never seen anyone who
resembled the handsome young man her mistress
described.

"Falcon is the toast of London," Bella boasted.
"He had five hundred guests at his coming-of-age
party, quite fifty of them French, for he spent a
year in Paris, you know. All my friends are in love
with him, especially the married ones!" And she
laughed.

Sabine was shocked, but fascinated. When
Roger Amhurst was finally bullied into submission
and the date of the visit drew near, her excitement made her feel almost sick as she wondered
if Falcon Amhurst would live up to the image
she had formed of him.

She watched with Bella as the carriages bowled
up the drive. "How do I look?" the other woman
asked anxiously, touching the fat little bunches
of curls she had insisted on wearing for the
occasion.

Sabine was deaf, her eyes intent on the drive-
way, wondering in which carriage Falcon
Amhurst was to be found.

Bella repeated the question petulantly, and
Sabine assured her eagerly that she looked very
well indeed, although she was really dubious
about those curls, and truthfully praised the rich
red of the gown she wore, which gave her sallow
complexion a rosier tinge and threw her black
hair into startling contrast.

Satisfied, Bella went down to welcome the
guests while Sabine peered over the stairs to
watch their arrival from a hidden vantage point.

There were six people, she saw: three young men in greatcoats, and two young ladies wrapped in mantles, while the last, a plump lady with a ludicrous feathered bonnet, was talking loudly as Roger Amhurst reluctantly embraced her.

"My dear Roger, how many years it is since we met! The journey . . . so wearisome . . . the roads are quite abominable. . . . How you have altered! I would not have known you. Quite altered. Poor dear Amelia. Such a sad event. That was the last time we met, I think. So charming of you to invite us . . . But Falcon, of course, being the heir . . . quite the thing for him to see the estate. And Bella. Dear Bella. What a pity you had to leave London. Such a shame that you never contrived to . . . hmm . . . discretion, yes, discretion!"

Both Bella and her brother were scarlet with anger and embarrassment by the time Mrs. Amhurst had been escorted into the house.

One of the young men, shedding his greatcoat and dropping it into the butler's outstretched hands, said lightly, "My dear Mama, so concerned with discretion and so indiscreet!" Then, bowing to Roger, "Cousin, I am happy to see you look so well. The country air clearly agrees with you."

Roger put out his hand. "Falcon. Good to see you," he said stiffly.

"Allow me to introduce my friends," said Falcon. "My sister, Fanny, you know, of course," waving towards a slight, pale girl with thick, dark hair, who curtseyed in silence. "And this is Philip Huntley, my closest friend. Philip is a retired army officer, y'know. Wounded at Waterloo and never in employment since. But a good fellow."

The man indicated, whose curling fair hair had already attracted Bella's interest, smiled but, like Fanny, said nothing.

"And this," said Falcon, turning to the last two of his party, "is George Grainger, son of Hartington Grainger, the banker." He glanced at the girl who stood close to George Grainger's shoulder as if for protection, "And his sister, Anne," he added, casually. "I beg your pardon, Anne. I had forgot you were there. . . ."

She blushed painfully, bobbing her head away like a shy little bird. She was very short, with mousy brown hair and big brown eyes, her manner nervous, and her clothes far too elaborate for someone of her height.

Bella, who had taken Mrs. Amhurst into the drawing room, came back with her and offered to lead the ladies to their rooms. Sabine hurriedly darted back to the little parlor and took up her sewing with a sigh. She was, of course, aware of her mistress's plans for Roger Amhurst, but had seen no one in the party who seemed to her to be suitable.

She had anticipated that she would see little of Bella Amhurst while the visitors were in the house, but next day when she entered the private parlor, she found her mistress there with Anne Grainger. Sabine flushed and curtseyed. "I am sorry. I thought . . ." she began, but Bella ordered her to come in and said to the other girl, "This is my maid, Sabine."

Anne Grainger looked surprised, as though she had never been introduced to a servant before, but smiled gently at Sabine.

"Sabine, will you mend Miss Grainger's stockings for her? She caught them on a nail."

Sabine took them and sat down in her accustomed chair. While she neatly darned the stockings, Bella calmly continued with her conversation.

She spoke of Sabine after a few moments, and mentioned her singing voice, which was very pretty. "Sing that country tune you sang for me the other day, Sabine," she ordered.

Sabine lay down the stocking, stood up and sang a little love song that was popular in her village. Her voice was clear and sweet, and her manner unaffected.

When she finished, Anne Grainger clapped her hands. "Oh, that was pretty, indeed," she said, so pleased that she forgot to be shy.

The door opened, and Falcon Amhurst's head appeared, his smile amused. "It was!" he agreed. "May I come in and join the company? I am bored with life downstairs. Your brother is interested in nothing but the slaughter of innocent animals, Bella."

Bella looked apologetic and murmured some vague reply.

He smiled and turned, his head cocked to one side, to stare at Sabine. "Is this the nightingale I heard just now?"

She was too shy to answer, and it was Bella who airily agreed that it had been Sabine who sang.

"Sabine," he murmured softly. "An odd name for a girl, surely?"

She lowered her eyes, flushing. Her mistress interrupted, her tone a little sharp, as though she disliked to see Sabine such a center of attraction.

"We were just going for a stroll, Falcon. Will you come?"

He immediately offered his arm, and they left the room, but as he closed the door behind him, his glance shot back at Sabine, his grin a little crooked, but friendly, and she felt a warmth glowing within her for some time afterwards.

Falcon Amhurst was twenty-three years old, but since he had been leading a free and lively existence since the age of seventeen, he had the sophistication and attitudes of a much older man. Tall and slim with an athletic build and hard muscles, he knew how to present a lounging appearance in polite drawing rooms, and he dressed in a dandy fashion that irritated Roger at once. His features were clean cut and chiselled. His nose was straight and perfectly balanced in proportion to his face, his eyes a vivid blue under the heavy black Amhurst brows which his cousin also possessed. In Falcon's case, however, there was a mocking, intimate droop to the lids on occasions, giving him a wryly personal look.

That evening the party assembled in the drawing room after supper and played cards and sang at the piano. Sabine could hear the rippling notes drifting up through the house, and she

sighed as she moved around Bella Amhurst's bedroom, picking up clothes and laying them away.

Next morning she was sent down to the village
with a parcel of old stockings for one of the
retired servants whom the Amhursts housed on
their estate. Walking back along the course of the
stream, she was taken aback to find Falcon Amhurst sitting on the bank on a stool, a hat pulled
down over his eyes, while a fishing rod was
propped up beside him. She tiptoed past nervously,
but as she was retreating, she heard a soft voice
behind her murmur, "Ah, the little nightingale!
Why are you creeping past me like a mouse?
Come here . . ."

She slowly turned back and saw his long face
watching her from beneath the shadow of his
hat, a humorous curve to his mouth. She curtseyed
and waited for him to speak.

"I have discovered that fishing is an excellent
excuse for doing nothing," he said, grinning. "But
now I am in a quandary, and you come just in
time to solve it for me." He waved his hand at a
basket which lay on the bank a few feet away.
"I brought provisions with me, as you see, but
am too idle to fetch them for myself. Will you
pour me a glass of wine, little nightingale?"

She thought him very idle, indeed, and her
firm little mouth tightened, but she obeyed without a word.

She found a glass resting in a nest of white
damask, but could see no bottle and glanced
round.

He waved a hand at the stream. "I hung it in the water to cool," he said.

She found the bottle, wiped it dry and poured a glass very carefully, then carried it to him.

He took it, raised it in a mocking salute, and sipped. "Oh, excellent," he said. "What more could one ask? A quiet pastoral spot, a pretty girl and a glass of wine?"

She curtseyed again and turned to go, but his free hand shot out and tethered her by the wrist. "Where are you off to? Come, I have heard you sing, let me hear you speak. Had I not heard you singing last night, I should have imagined you as dumb as an ox."

"I have my duties to attend to, sir," she said, resentful of his mockery.

"Ah, duty," he murmured. "My cousin Roger uses that word so often it must be threadbare. And what are your duties, child?"

"I wait upon Miss Bella," she said crossly. "I help her to dress, mend her clothes, pick them up when she lets them fall and make her new ones when they wear out." And her big, blue-green eyes stared defiantly at him.

He grimaced. "It sounds precious dull to me. And do you like your duties, child?"

Her tone was pitying, as though she spoke to an idiot, "Like them or not, sir, that is what I am paid to do, and it must be done."

His face suddenly relaxed into a smile so charming that she blinked. "I stand rebuked. You must excuse my ill manners. The truth is I have never seen a servant girl in London with your beauty. You could earn a fortune with that voice in the London theaters, you know, especially as you are so pretty."

She looked shocked. "An actress, sir? Oh, I could not. It is not a life for a decent girl."

His lids drooped again, and that quizzical curve returned to his long mouth. "No? Perhaps you are right. You are probably happier here. Well, run along, child, and do your duty. But you must sing for me again some time. Such a voice should not be hid."

When she returned to the house, she found her mistress sitting in her parlor with her two female visitors, Anne Grainger and Fanny Amhurst, drinking tea and chattering together.

Bella Amhurst turned and said sharply, "You took long enough to walk to the village, girl. My bedroom is in a shocking state. Attend to it now, will you, and do not let me see it like that again!" And as Sabine, hot-faced and angry, went out, Bella said to the other girls, "These country wenches are so idle! One needs to be watching them all day, or nothing gets done!"

Sabine found the bedroom in total disarray. It looked as if Miss Amhurst had flung her entire wardrobe about the room and left it where it fell. Stockings, petticoats, gowns and ribbons were strewn everywhere. Sighing, Sabine rapidly returned it to its usual condition and then went down to eat dinner in the servants' hall.

The squire, feeling that he had done his duty as a host in spending their first evening under his roof with his guests, relapsed into his old ways that evening and retired early to his gun room with a bottle of brandy.

Mrs. Amhurst ate her way greedily through a vast supper, then pleaded a headache and went to her room to sleep it off, leaving the young people in the drawing room.

"I count you a perfectly adequate chaperone," she told Bella coyly as she left.

Bella, flushed and angry, did not reply. She did not yet count herself on the shelf and was hopeful of the pleasant young retired officer, Captain Huntley, who had been paying her some attentions.

He led her to the piano and begged her to play to them, which she was happy to do, while Falcon lounged in a chair and stared at the clock, and the two Graingers whispered to Fanny Amhurst who sat between them on the sofa turning over a book of prints.

"Will you sing for us?" Captain Huntley asked Bella.

She shook her head, smiling. "I have a weak singing voice, I am afraid."

The young man exchanged a secret glance with Falcon over her head, grinned at him, and then said to Bella, "Miss Grainger has been praising your little maid to us all day. Is it true she sings superbly? I wish I could hear her. Your playing and her voice must make an irresistible combination."

Anne Grainger, who admired Captain Huntley, at once supported him enthusiastically. "Oh, do let her be sent for to sing! My brother would so much like to hear her! That simple country style of singing is all the rage in London at present."

Bella was not pleased by this request but wished to fall in with anything desired by Captain Huntley, and so she rang for the butler and informed him that Sabine was needed in the drawing room.

This stately gentleman looked as shocked as his wooden face could permit but withdrew obediently, and a few moments later Sabine, in a clean blue gown and white cap, arrived, flushed and uneasy.

Bella informed her that she was needed to sing, with stilted artificiality that barely masked a deep irritation.

Sabine had never before sung to so many people and was very nervous, but Captain Huntley gave her a comforting smile and begged her to sing the song she had already sung to Miss Grainger. Miss Amhurst picked up the tune easily and followed her with deft fingers. When Sabine's last clear note ended, the young people clapped with great enthusiasm.

"There," said Miss Grainger to her brother, "did I say too much?"

"She sings beautifully," he admitted, and asked if she knew a more cheerful song.

Sabine had had no musical training and could only sing the simple traditional tunes she had learned in her childhood, so she sang another of these, a lively, jolly tune usually sung at harvest suppers when the men were merry with cider.

"Well done," called Mr. Grainger loudly, stamping his feet until his sister pinched his arm warningly.

Falcon had watched Sabine closely as she sang, and she, although never once glancing in his direction, had been aware of his gaze. As she left the room again, she passed his chair, and their eyes met. He was leaning back idly, his long legs stretched out, his blue eyes half-hooded by those heavy lids. His expression was wry, as though he had strange thoughts, and she sensed that she herself had some connection with those thoughts.

Bella Amhurst said jealously, "You think her pretty, Captain Huntley?"

He shrugged. "For a country girl, I suppose she is—but her looks will not last. They never do with these girls. In two years her bloom will have gone, and she will be coarse-skinned and brown, like a gypsy."

Bella's face relaxed. "You must describe to me what you saw at the battle of Waterloo," she cooed, gazing up at him. "You must have been very brave, Captain. They say the casualties were high."

"Far too high," he admitted, frowning, and talked lightly of his own experiences.

Philip Huntley on leaving the army, had had no notion of what he intended to do with the rest of his life and, living on a very small income, had grown weary of cutting his coat to suit his cloth.

On Falcon's advice, he had attempted to engage the affections of various wealthy young ladies but had always come up against the insuperable obstacle of their indignant families. "There is nothing for it, then," Falcon had said at last. "We must become relations."

"Relations?" Philip had repeated, smiling. Falcon always amused him, and there was a strong bond of affection between them, although Philip could give Falcon at least ten years.

"Do you dislike the notion?" Falcon had drawled, raising one flippant eyebrow.

"Not entirely," Philip had retorted. "Were I related to you, I should feel myself free to give you the whipping you undoubtedly deserve."

"You could always try," Falcon had grinned.

"You refer, I presume, to your sister?" Philip had gone on, frowning. "I have never seen any sign of interest in me there, my dear fellow."

"Not Fanny," Falcon said idly. "My cousin, Arabella Amhurst, I mean—she is a trifle horse-faced, and very dull, but she has a fortune of her own and is thirty years old and therefore of an age to choose for herself. You must remember meeting her."

Philip shook his head. "The description is hardly encouraging, but it rings no bells with me. Why should you imagine she would be agreeable to my suit?"

"Because, my dear good fellow, she is at the age of desperation and would take Satan himself, tail and all."

Philip had grimaced. "I do not know if I am yet so desperate myself, however. You do not exactly paint an alluring prospect, Falcon."

"It is best to be frank at the start. You must marry, Philip, and Bella is not ill-natured if she is treated right. She has invited me to bring some friends down to stay at Ceorlbury. You might as well come along and take a look at her. If you dislike her, by all means cry off. But you will not meet a better prospect. Love and money rarely come together."

Philip was an easygoing, pleasant young man. He had shrugged and accepted Falcon's advice in the end. He was not unaware that he carried his fortune in his person, being fair and slim with a certain elegance about him. He had aged well and did not show his thirty-three years, but he was a little bored with his bachelor life and was ready to settle down, especially if the bride could gild the domestic nest sufficiently to make it very comfortable.

Now, as he talked easily to Bella, he was thinking that she would not be unacceptable as a wife. He could not pretend to any passion for her. She was all that Falcon had described. But, since Falcon had been so brutally frank at the start, Philip was left with a feeling of relief, since Bella had some virtues which Falcon had not mentioned. True, she was not pretty, but she would look better if she chose her gowns more carefully. Philip's taste in dress was acute, and he felt he could improve Bella's appearance easily enough by persuading her to wear more vivid colors.

He had become slightly cynical since leaving the army where the constant presence of death bred a certain dark gaiety but brought out men's true natures, and one could know one's friends.

He could not live on air, and the faint *tendresse* he felt for one girl of his acquaintance could never come to fruition as she barely seemed to know he existed.

There seemed no reason why he should not marry Bella as Falcon advised.

Bella, meanwhile, was hungrily observing him in her turn. In London their paths had not crossed often, but when they had, she had noticed him with interest. Her dark eyes lingered on his face, wondering what it would feel like to stroke the thick, fair curls which clustered so casually upon his head.

Alert to every expression of their faces, Falcon watched, thinking that Philip had, as he had suspected for some time, made a conquest in Bella. If he wanted her fortune, he would be too sensible to jib at her hysterical temper, but Falcon hoped Bella would not reveal herself too clearly until Philip was hooked.

Pity the little nightingale has no fortune, he thought, sighing. Are her eyes green or blue, I wonder? What a lovely face she has, as clear as well water. And a mouth like a rose, pink and soft and very inviting. Now if she had not been a servant, I would feel myself in danger. And the hooded eyes drooped lower in self-contempt. I must not think of her. It would only lead to disaster.

CHAPTER TWO

Since both Bella Amhurst and Captain Huntley had very good reasons for desiring to marry each other, their courtship was soon accomplished without any of the delicate preliminaries usual in these cases, and he was able to declare his position openly to her after a very short time.

She pretended surprise and protested that he must speak to her brother, while showing her own delight in every look and gesture. She was determined that Roger Amhurst should give his permission but was afraid that he would be difficult to persuade into such an act. Roger had no great liking for the gallant captain.

Philip pressed her hand. "But you have no dislike of the idea yourself?" he urged, eager to have a clear commitment on her side.

She returned the pressure of his fingers, smiling, and he was satisfied.

Roger, meanwhile, had heard his guests discussing Sabine, and, frowning, sent for her to his library where he ordered her to sing for him. Flustered and embarrassed by his scowl, she obeyed, and he listened in a grim silence.

When she faltered into the last phrase, he stared at her, leaning back in his chair, his face shuttered and dark.

"Aye," he said reluctantly. "It's a pretty voice. But I do not like to hear my servants talked of in my own drawing room. Be wary of London gentlemen, child. They are not to be trusted."

She flushed. "I am sorry, sir."

"It is not your fault. My sister brought you to their attention. But guard yourself against them. They will take you up for their amusement and do you nothing but harm."

She stared at the floor, twisting her hands.

"You understand me?"

"Yes, sir," she whispered.

He hesitated, then went on heavily, "If you get yourself into trouble, I shall not lift a finger for you. You are old enough to know what is right and what is wrong. Trust none of them. Eh?"

"Yes, sir," she said again, curtseyed, and went out to walk in the park for half an hour to cool her hot face and calm her nerves.

In one of the wooded paths, she met Falcon Amhurst who had come out to escape from his cousin's continual talk of the estate. Roger, having Falcon under Ceorlbury's roof, meant to drum into the young man's head that he was heir to a great estate and should learn as much as he could of the management of it. His own passionate love for the land blinded him to Falcon's indifference.

"You should marry again, Roger," Falcon said when his cousin talked of his inheritance.

Indignantly, Roger said, "I do not wish to— you will serve as my heir in the due course of events. I do not mean to die yet, you know, but you should be prepared for the event. You should come out with me and learn something of what is to be done."

"It sounds like a great deal of labor from what you say," Falcon drawled.

"It is a satisfying task," Roger said enthusiastically. "One has to be master of many subjects. There is the timber, for instance. That brings in a good income and needs constant care. And the farms must be kept in repair. Then there is the stream—I keep it well stocked for my own use. Jabez is a good bailiff, but the master should know every inch of his land better than any hired man."

Falcon yawned. "I am sure you are right, my dear Roger, but you forget one thing."

Roger halted, stared. "Oh?"

"I am town born and bred. I know nothing of the country. What use would I be to Ceorlbury? No, you must marry and get yourself an heir more suited to the duty than myself."

Roger's face darkened. "You cannot be serious."

"I am rarely serious," Falcon said lightly. "But on this occasion, I am in deadly earnest."

"You do not want to inherit?" repeated Roger, dumbfounded and horrified.

"Not on these terms. I quite liked the idea until I saw in how serious a light you took your duties, but since I did not intend to live here, I feel I should warn you of my intentions and give you a chance to replace me with another heir."

"Good heavens, man, you must be mad!" roared Roger, dark red with rage. "How can you talk so to me?"

"I owe it to you to be honest," Falcon said, smiling that wry smile of his.

"You are insolent, young man," Roger retorted. "I have a good mind to take you at your word."

"Do so, cousin," Falcon added gently before leaving him to think over what had been said.

But as he walked among the newly leaved trees, hearing their branches sighing in the wind with such a musical sound, he wondered if he had not been too hasty in declaring himself to Roger. He had come down to Ceorlbury thoughtlessly, aware of the position in which he stood, but having given it little consideration. The first few days had shown him how seriously Roger took the duties which should fall upon the master of the estate, and he had been alarmed by the thought of burying himself in the remote countryside for the rest of his life, going through the dull rounds of a squire's life.

Now, however, having attempted to burn his boats behind him, he had a brief flash of regret. There was much to be said for life in the country, he thought, gazing up into the branches where a wood pigeon was idiotically cooing. The mild air cooled his face, refreshing him, and he sauntered on slowly, feeling soothed and at rest.

This was a very beautiful part of the world. The earth seemed to turn more slowly on its axis, the seasons to melt imperceptibly, the constant beauty of the landscape to wonder and amaze the eye.

Another human figure appeared before him, moving gracefully over the grass, and he felt a

queer little throb of emotion as he realized that
it was the little nightingale herself.

She halted as she saw him, her eyes widening
in surprise. He stared at them closely and saw
that they were neither green nor blue, but a mixture of both.

She looked perfectly at ease in this rural setting,
her simple gown and sweet face the right comple-
ment for the beauty around her.

She looked around as if seeking some escape,
and he quickly walked towards her to block her
path.

Looking down from his greater height, he
smiled, and her cheeks grew very pink.

"Why are you so frightened of me?" he asked
lightly. "Every time I see you, I seem to terrify
you."

She did not know how to answer this, having no
experience of flirtation, and so did not speak at
all.

He grimaced. "You are a close little creature,
aren't you? I never met a woman who said less.
Tell me, where did you get that odd name of
yours? I never heard it before."

"My father gave it me," she said uncomfort-
ably, conscious of the warning the squire had so
recently given her against the London visitors.

"And who was your father?"

"A shepherd over to Twyne Abbas," she said,
deliberately emphasizing her rural burr.

The hooded lids drooped, and a little smile
twitched at the corners of his mouth, as if he
knew why she spoke with such a country accent.

"How came he by such a name for you?" he asked, aware of a strong desire to keep her talking.

"He was book-learned. He did say it was an old Roman name or something, but I don't know what exactly."

He watched the curve of her soft cheek, the lift of her opalescent eyes, the dimples which came and went as she spoke. She fascinated him, and he wondered what would become of her in the future. With such beauty, she must have many yokel suitors. A nerve flickered in his cheek at the thought. It was revolting even to consider the idea of this lovely creature yoked with some stupid cowherd or gardener. There was clear intelligence in those eyes which must make her too good for any such fellow.

"Have you never heard the story, then?" he asked, aware that she must be interested and wishing to keep her with him for as long as possible.

She looked up, surprised. "Story? What story?" Then, remembering her position, "Sir."

"For heaven's sake," he said, in a flash of irritation. "Call me Falcon or Mr. Amhurst, but not that eternal 'sir,' as though I were a graybeard or a parson."

She looked shocked. "You are a guest in my master's house, sir."

He grimaced. "Yes, yes. Well, the story." He sensed that she was again wary of him and wanted to distract her quickly, so he plunged into the story of the rape of the Sabine women by the lonely Romans.

She listened with deep interest, frowning, and when he had finished, said, "They were wicked men, then, those Romans?" And, to herself, as if forgetting his presence, "That's what the squire meant, then."

"Why? What did he say?"

"That I would make even the sternest Roman forget the path of righteousness," she replied simply, then blushed as she realized to whom she spoke. "Oh, I'm sorry, sir . . . excuse me . . ."

"Why apologize? It was my cousin who made the remark, not you. But he was right." And absently, he reached out and touched the soft curve of her cheek, feeling the tiny golden hairs like peach bloom under his fingers.

She was very still, staring up like a hypnotized bird at a snake, her pink lips slightly parted.

Falcon sighed deeply, bent his head, and his mouth touched hers, lightly, caressingly. Her lips opened on a sigh, and his kiss lingered, gentle and sensitive, then he lifted his head and smiled wryly at her.

"I am sorry, my dear. You are far too pretty for your own good, or my peace of mind."

She stared, very flushed, picked up her skirts and ran back towards the house in a fluster of excitement and apprehension. Falcon's kiss had awakened in her a realization of how attractive he was and of the needs she had never hitherto understood. It had been her first kiss, and she was not disappointed in it. He had kissed with just the sensitivity a first kiss should hold, neither frightening nor demanding too much. But although she had enjoyed that kiss, it alarmed her in retrospect. He was a gentleman. One of the lighthearted London men the squire had warned her against. The tones of that warning stood in her mind, and she shivered. She knew what getting into trouble meant. It meant an unwanted baby and an outcast mother. Falcon Amhurst was a handsome young man, and she found him very attractive, but she would keep away from him in the future.

Captain Huntley, meanwhile, was having his interview with an icy Squire of Ceorlbury. Roger paced the room, his back stiff with indignation. "You have nothing to offer but yourself, sir, and I see no reason why you should be so attractive a proposition to my family. My sister tells me she favors your suit. Well, I will be blunt—I do not and never shall."

Flushed to the fair curls upon his forehead, the captain said, "I cannot pretend to be surprised, sir. I have no right to address Miss Amhurst, but . . ."

Roger broke in angrily, "Do not tell me you are madly in love with Bella, for I am too sly to be caught by such honeyed talk. You may fool her. She's a damned fool at the best of times. But I am not to be sweet-talked into believing such a lie."

Captain Huntley attempted to turn the tide, but his host was brutally downright, and at last he left with a grim face, and rejoined the waiting lady with a look of resignation.

"He will not agree," he said flatly.

She shrieked. "I knew how it would be! He

wishes me to die an old maid. He will not marry again himself and wishes no one else to do so! He is the most detestable, selfish man . . ." she paused, seeing Philip's expression, and moderated her tones to a sweeter note, "Oh, how can I bear it! My dearest Philip! We must and shall be married!"

He was not so certain now that he wished it. Her hysterical reaction had reminded him rather too strongly of her brother.

She clasped his hand, sighing and rolling her eyes, like a lovesick dog. "We will elope," she said ardently.

He backed, frowning. "I do not think that wise. It will cause such a scandal. I would not wish your name bandied about in the London clubs. . . ."

"I will take Sabine with me," she said eagerly, clutching at his arm in desperation. "That will be sufficient to make it respectable."

He was still unwilling, but after she had talked to him for some time, he allowed himself to be persuaded. He could see that she was quite determined, and his good nature made it hard for him to wound her by balking at this fence.

"But I wish to God you had never suggested this," he told Falcon. "If you had seen her when I told her how her brother had refused me—she was positively screaming with rage. If I had had the courage, I should have run off, but I was afraid she would run mad altogether if I did."

"She is easy enough to handle," Falcon drawled. "She dotes upon you already, and you will be happy enough. You cannot live in poverty, my dear Philip."

"No," Philip agreed. "That is a powerful argument, too. But I wish that you would come with us, Falcon."

Falcon laughed, his eyes amused, "On an elopement? I would be somewhat *de trop,* I fancy."

"I shall need a support."

"Two is company, three is none," his friend retorted.

"She is bringing her maid, anyway, as a chaperone," Philip explained. "And as you are her cousin, it would give more of a look of respectability to the affair."

Falcon was thoughtful. "I see. Well, in that case. . . ."

Philip clapped him upon the back. "Thank you, Falcon—I'll do the same for you, one day."

When Sabine was informed, late the next evening, that she was to accompany her mistress on an elopement that very night, she was aghast. "You must not do it, ma'am," she blurted out.

Bella turned an angry face upon her. "You can hold your tongue! Captain Huntley is an officer of the highest repute, and if my brother is stupid enough to dislike him, I cannot help it. I shall marry him at all costs." Bella's breath caught roughly, "I love him," she stammered, wishing to say it aloud even if only to a maid.

Sabine was silenced. She had seen the desperation in her mistress's sallow face, and she guessed at the depth of sincerity behind her words.

As they furtively prepared to leave, Bella said softly, "Is it not strange? I arranged this visit in order to find a wife for my brother, and I find myself a husband. I was ten years in London with one or another of my aunts, hoping to find a husband, and then within a short time of returning home in despair, I meet Philip! Is he not handsome, Sabine?"

"Very, ma'am," said the maid innocently.

"And charming!"

"Yes, indeed, ma'am," said Sabine, with disguised pity. She suspected that Captain Huntley was a fortune hunter and feared that Bella would regret her decision later, but she saw that nothing she or anyone else could say would move the other woman. And it was better that Sabine should be there with her than that Bella should go alone.

They slipped silently down the back stairs and out into the darkened stable yard, where the only sound was the occasional snort from one of the horses or a stamping of their feet as they moved around restlessly.

Falcon and Captain Huntley were waiting there and greeted them in a whisper. "The carriage is waiting at the end of the drive," Falcon said.

Sabine, who had been unaware that Falcon was to be one of the party, was surprised and shocked to see him. That he should encourage his cousin to marry a fortune hunter said little for his own sense of responsibility.

Bella clutched at Captain Huntley's arm and walked ahead with him, whispering in his ear.

Sabine followed, carrying the two bags they had packed, ignoring Falcon, who stalked along beside her for a moment in silence before taking the bags from her without a word.

The sky was as calm as a mill pond, the soft purple of ripe grapes, and stars glittered against its breast like crystallized tears. There was no wind. A great stillness lay everywhere in the hushed park.

Sabine had a feeling of apprehension. She was convinced that what they were doing was wrong. Sad and heavy of step she walked behind Bella and Captain Huntley, watching their heads close together, hearing the hushed whispering of their voices in the still night.

What sort of man was he, this quiet, friendly gentleman who had persuaded a woman to defy her family and elope with him? He looked so pleasant, yet his actions spoke of him as a scoundrel. And he was Falcon Amhurst's dearest friend!

Falcon moved close to her. "What are you thinking?" he asked in that drawling, intimate voice of his, peering under the brim of her bonnet.

She was grateful for the protection of the darkness. "I sir?" she said in assumed simplicity. "Nothing, sir."

He laughed softly. "You are enchanting," he said. Then, after a pause, "Shall you go with them to London as Bella's maid? Or shall you return to Ceorlbury?"

Sadly, she said, "Squire would not take me back after I had aided his sister to elope. I do not know what I shall do."

He was silent. She could not know that he was thinking how much he would like to take her away, alone, to some remote spot where the fashionable world never penetrated, and he could be alone with her for months on end. He grimaced and shook his head silently. Such thoughts were indefensible. He could not marry her, and he would ruin her entirely if he followed his own wishes.

Aloud, he said, "If you went back now and told my cousin of his sister's plan, he would forgive you."

"I couldn't do that," she said indignantly, "That would be . . . rank treachery!"

He smiled. "Strange, honest, little creature, how all occasions do inform against you!"

She was baffled. "Sir?"

"Mere folly. Forget it." And they walked on in total silence until they reached the carriage. Then she climbed in after her mistress; the two men followed, and the carriage moved slowly forward, leaving Ceorlbury behind sleeping in the great silent park.

Captain Huntley and Bella Amhurst were married a week later by special license in London and returned after the ceremony to their lodgings for a wedding breakfast with Falcon and Sabine. There had been no other friends or relatives at the short service, but Bella was glowing with delight as she clung to Philip's hand.

Sabine was shyly uneasy at Captain Huntley's insistence that she be a guest at the meal, but Bella supported him eagerly, "You shall sit down with us, Sabine. I insist. You have been my friend throughout, and I am very grateful." She poured Sabine a glass of wine and kissed her on the cheek. "Come, drink our health! You and Falcon are the only guests, you know. We could not lose you or our little party would be even smaller."

Sabine drank, blinking at the unaccustomed taste, and Falcon watched with tender amusement as her small nose wrinkled in involuntary distaste.

There was a piano in their lodgings, and they sat around it, listening to Bella playing while Philip Huntley filled their glasses again and again, his own countenance flushed.

"Sabine shall sing for us," he insisted, and Bella played the accompaniment while Sabine sang several of her country songs.

The wine had given heat to Philip's blood. He caught his new wife by the hand and whispered to her, bringing a new wave of color to her cheek.

They went to the door, saying good night on the way, and vanished.

Sabine rose, too, and began automatically to tidy the room. Her own sleeping quarters were in a narrow cupboard at the very top of the house, but before she went to bed she felt she should make the effort to set their shared parlor to rights.

Falcon watched her lazily for a little while, then caught at her hand as she passed him. "That is enough. Let the servants do the rest tomorrow. We are paying through the nose for these lodgings, anyway."

Very conscious of the dazed effect of the wine upon her mind, she tried to withdraw her fingers from his grasp, but his hand tightened like a vise.

"No," he said, thickly. "You are so lovely, Sabine . . ." and pulled her down until she fell across his lap.

She tried to struggle up again, but his arms had slipped around her, and he was bending his head to kiss her mouth.

Confused thoughts filled her brain. This is dangerous, she thought frantically, pushing against his chest, but the wine had done its work too well. She could no longer think clearly, especially as his mouth moved hungrily closer, and his hands slid up and down her back, pressing her nearer to him.

Her emotions conquered her common sense. She felt her spine yielding, her limbs growing heavy and weak as though in sleep, and unconsciously her arms crept up around his neck, reaching to the base of his head, where the black hair curled inward upon his nape.

Falcon had not intended what followed. He was not given to the seduction of innocence and, aware of his growing attraction towards Sabine, had meant to keep a tight rein upon his actions. But the conjunction of their presence alone at night and the overindulgence in wine overthrew all his good intentions.

Next morning he left before anyone was awake, burning with self-reproach and shame, and Sabine, on discovering his absence, was stricken into panic.

Now that the heady weakness of abandonment had passed, she saw herself with clarity. So much

for the squire's warning, she thought miserably. He
was right about gentlemen. But what was she to
do now? She was too humiliated to stay with
Captain and Mrs. Huntley, where, at any time,
she might meet Falcon again. She did not know
anyone in London, and her father was too far
away in Yorkshire to be of any help to her, even
supposing that he would wish to help.

Her instinct, like that of a wounded animal, was
to bolt for home. But she had no home except
Ceorlbury, and the squire would not want her
there.

Bella, when she heard of Sabine's decision to
leave her, was very angry. "I have just trained you
in my ways! It will be most inconvenient if you
leave. I shall not give you a reference, I warn
you."

But Captain Huntley later sought Sabine out
and gently questioned her. He had some suspicions
of Falcon's interest in her, and her burning face
when he mentioned his friend convinced him that
Falcon's sudden disappearance without warning
had some bearing upon Sabine's decision to leave
her mistress.

He was a kindly if rather weak man, and he
was shocked by what he suspected. Falcon's
affairs with actresses and ladies of the demimonde
were only to be expected in London society, but
the seduction of an innocent country girl seemed
to him to be cruelly selfish.

"You must go back to Dorset if you wish it,"
he told her gently, "Take these . . ." and pressed
into her hand some guineas, "I will give you a

reference myself." He sat down and quickly wrote a glowing letter of recommendation. "There, child. I hope you find a good place. I should go at once. My wife will not miss you until you are well on your way."

He took Bella out shopping for new gowns while Sabine packed her few pitiful belongings and set out to take the coach back to Dorset.

On arrival at Dorchester, she took the first post she was offered, as a serving maid in a lodging house in the town, but she could not settle in her new place. Dorchester's narrow alleys and noisy bustle made her homesick for the silence of the sheepfolds on the eweleaze at Twynehams, and the chatter and insolence of the men who came to sleep at the house made her shrink into herself.

One morning she woke feeling slightly sick, and a suspicion darkened her mind.

She sat up and thought back over the last six weeks. Her face whitened in shock. Surely it could not be true, she thought in panic.

But as the next few days passed, she realized that her fears were only too well founded. She was to have Falcon Amhurst's child.

She twisted and turned like a rabbit in a trap, sickened and horrified by the realization. She did not know what to do and dared confide in no one.

There seemed to be no escape from the shame that must follow. Unmarried mothers were outcasts in her world. She would be turned out of her place at the lodging house and left to fend for herself. There was only one place in Dorchester where someone in her condition could go—and one evening she tremblingly ventured near it to see for herself what she had only heard of from drunken men at the lodging house returning from an evening's entertainment there.

The dark alley was silent, but she could see, when she peered along its length, pale shadows of women loitering in the doorways, waiting for their visitors.

They caught sight of her and gave a chorus of jeering comments upon her, terrifying her so much that she scuttled away, her face damp with perspiration, shivering as though she had the ague.

She would never permit herself to sink to that level, she decided in horror.

Next day she stole out of the lodging house early in the morning while everyone still slept and, leaving her few small possessions behind her, set out to walk to Ceorlbury.

She could not have said what it was that drew her to the house in which she had first met Falcon. Some dim feeling of revenge hovered at the back of her mind.

She had decided to kill herself rather than face the shame that must come, and she chose to do this at Ceorlbury, where the news of it must come to the ears of the man responsible for her fate.

It was dusk when she reached the park wall, and she walked round until she came to the low arched bridge which spanned the stream. Below this the waters fell over a rocky place, joining with another little stream to form a wider expanse of water which rushed down fast over the valley floor, foaming and leaping up the green banks. There had been much rain in the past week, and the river ran above its usual level.

Sabine sat down and stared into the water. The air around her was sweet with flower scents, and the earth was moist beneath her feet, but she was only conscious of her misery.

She watched the dark water steadily as it rushed past, making the river ferns tremble and the tall reeds whisper. It seemed to her to be like her own life, which had passed so swiftly that she had not understood any moment of it until now. She had lived from moment to moment, without reflection or desire, going where the tide of circumstance carried her. But now she had come up against a parting of the ways, and she must make a conscious and personal choice.

With a sigh, she stepped down off the bank into the cold water, shivered as its chill soaked through her clothes and felt her breath catch sharply in her chest.

But she would not turn back now. She clenched herself against her own weakness and walked on while the water rose higher against her, swirling around, pulling at her like dark hands.

Her full skirts rose up, belling outwards, and floated on the water, which was now level with her chest and lapped, at each step, upwards to her chin.

She looked up at the sky, shuddering. It rolled overhead in a dark turbulence, cloudy and wind-fretted. The moon was not yet up, and the sun had long since set.

Her teeth chattered against each other. Angry with herself for her hesitation now, she let herself fall backward, her arms flying up into the air, and the icy water took her.

CHAPTER THREE

Roger Amhurst had been restless too that evening and had walked for hours, his head sunk down upon his chest, his spaniel, Coll, padding silently after him.

His sister's elopement had broken up the house party. Roger had savagely ordered Falcon Amhurst's mother and sister to take the other guests back to London. "He shall regret this, madam," he roared at Mrs. Amhurst. "My sister is a fool, and your son is a scoundrel! I believe he plotted this from the start with that penniless fortune-hunting friend of his! Well, I cannot prevent Bella having her inheritance, but neither she nor her husband shall ever set foot in my house again, and neither, madam, shall your son."

Flustered and angry, she retorted, "You cannot cut him out of the entailment, you know. He must inherit."

"Have you considered, madam, that my sister may have a son?" shouted Roger in a mixture of triumph and bitterness.

Mrs. Amhurst had not, and her expression betrayed her startled apprehension. Roger laughed viciously.

"Oh, yes, if she does, then it will be her child who will inherit Ceorlbury, not yours! I almost hope she does. It would be a fitting revenge upon your son, madam!"

Mrs. Amhurst drove back to London with a burning desire to whip her son as he had never been whipped in his childhood. How could he throw away his inheritance, she thought furiously. The fool!

Roger, relapsing into his usual way of life, had been torn between conflicting emotions ever since.

He now loathed Falcon, who had so casually shrugged off the inheritance which he should have been proud to own. Roger could not forget the frivolous way in which Falcon had talked of Ceorlbury.

For generations their family had lived on this land, loving and tending it, and Roger's own life had been built upon this deep emotional bond with the earth on which his sheep grazed and his ploughs ran. Yet his heir, who would inherit rolling acres as green and fertile as any in the kingdom, could only protest indifference to the idea of living here!

Their ancestors must be turning in their quiet graves. Roger had walked there and stood gazing heavily at the mossy graves of long-dead Amhursts, wondering if he himself would be the last of the family to be buried there.

A bitter prospect stretched before him. Either Falcon would inherit and squander his income in London while Ceorlbury slowly died for lack of care, or Bella would bear a son to her opportunist husband, and that child would inherit.

Roger had not liked Captain Huntley. He had

been too smooth and plausible for Roger's rough country taste. His son would probably be another of that sort.

What a damnable thought, he told himself furiously. Either one of them would ruin the estate. They would feed upon it like vultures until it was nothing but bare bones.

There was, of course, a third possibility. Roger himself could marry and attempt to get an heir.

He frowned savagely, kicking at tufts of grass. His first wife had been a widow when he married her and had, during her first marriage, borne a son who had died in infancy. Nevertheless, it had proved her capable of conception, whereas Roger had no such proof of his own powers. He had had brief affairs with local women from time to time, hoping that he might manage to prove to himself that he was able to father a child, but without success.

The very thought of marrying again and failing once more to have children made him grow hot and cold with embarrassment and wounded pride. He would rather see a stranger at Ceorlbury than make himself a public show by marrying again and conspicuously failing to get a child.

He was now some way from the house, outside the park, and he turned down a sunken lane which ran between two fields under hedges thick with flowers. It was almost night. The moths were beginning to flit between the trees, and there was a faint mist rising from the damp banks.

He found himself walking under the willows which drooped above the river bank. Brushing aside their leafy branches when they touched his face, he walked on, his mind tossing between savage rage and pessimistic resignation.

The spaniel which had fallen a little behind stopped suddenly, whining, and Roger halted to look back at him.

"What is it, sir? A rat? Come, Coll. Leave the damned thing be! Hell, I tell you, sir, leave it and come to me!"

The dog, staring downstream with rigid attention, whining softly, paid him no heed. The banks were full of water rats, the soft earth honeycombed with their nests, and Roger watched the water closely, expecting to see the telltale fanning ripple that would betray a swimming rat. Then he, too, heard a sound. Muffled, faint, like a groan.

Was there something out there, in the very middle of the stream, a struggling shape beating about? The moon had not come up, and he could only see vaguely, but on a sudden impulse he threw off his coat and boots and struck out into the cold current.

Coll, barking excitedly now, leapt in after him, head up and paws paddling wildly.

Sabine was too possessed with shock to be consciously aware of what was happening. Her lungs were choked with water, and when strong hands seized her, she fought and kicked against them instinctively, tenaciously holding to the idea that had first sent her into the stream. She was no longer capable of knowing what she did, but that deeper part of her mind which dictated unconscious action made her fight to die.

Roger, as instinctively, struck her a blow upon the chin with a balled fist. Then, with difficulty, he dragged and pulled her half-drowned, sodden body to the bank, heaved her upwards and himself followed.

Coll scrambled up after them and began shaking himself with vigor.

Returning to consciousness in a fit of shuddering nausea, Sabine was sprayed in the face by the water from the dog's thick coat and gasped.

Her throat seemed to ache intolerably. Its muscles were scraped and sore, and she spoke with pain, "Oh, why did you not leave me to die?" The cry was frail with anguish.

Roger did not answer. He had not yet recognized in this wet, bedraggled object the lovely child who had sung her simple country songs to him so recently.

"Can you walk?" he asked abruptly. "There is a hut near here where we will find shelter. Come, give me your arm, and I will help you."

The hut was one once occupied by one of the gardeners. Built of wood, roofed in thatch, it was now in a state of decay and had been allowed to run to ruin, but the thatch was still in place, although nibbled by mice and pitted with birds' nests, and there were still various domestic articles within since it was sometimes used by itinerant laborers at harvest time.

Roger carried her within and laid her, fainting, on an old straw palliasse on the floor. Then he fumbled about until he found a lantern on a hook and lit the candle with his tinderbox. There was a feeling of dampness about the unused building, and mice scrambled away out of sight at this sudden appearance of light.

On one side of the hut stood a brazier. Roger found some dry straw and sticks of kindling and, with some puffing and judicious tending, managed to light a creditable fire.

The spaniel, damp tail thumping, crept close to the brazier and lay down, his dark eyes fixed unwinkingly on it.

The smoke from the fire rose into the hut, so that Roger coughed and quickly opened the shutters on a rough window above the brazier. Without looking at the girl, the squire moved about the hut, looking on the shelves which had been crudely hung on the walls. He took down a battered saucepan and went out again into the night. A moment later he returned and placed the saucepan, now full of water, on an iron ring which he swung out over the fire.

Then, taking down the swinging lantern, he crossed to the palliasse and looked down at the girl who lay with closed eyes, every line of her body indicating dejection and misery.

He stood transfixed, staring at her, the lantern raised to illumine her face. A stern look hardened his eyes. His lips came together in a hard line.

Turning away again, he found an old horse blanket in a mildewed wooden chest. He threw it towards her. "Take off your wet clothes and wrap yourself in this."

Then he turned his back on her and began to make tea with the hot water in the saucepan. In a series of wooden canisters, he found some dusty grains of tea, a lump of damp, coarse, brown sugar and other old provisions. He deftly busied himself with these while Sabine struggled up obediently and stripped off her wet clothes. When she was rolled in the blanket, she sat up on the edge of the palliasse, watching his back.

"Are you done?" he asked curtly.

"Yes, sir," she whispered.

He turned and put the wet objects on a rope which hung along the wall above the brazier. The previous tenants of this place had clearly often dried wet clothes in just such a way, for they hung so that the drops falling from them did not drop into the fire.

He had made the tea in a rusty iron can. Now he poured it, hot, black and sweet, into two chipped earthenware mugs and came over to her with one.

She accepted it with a bent head and sipped gratefully enough. The tea warmed and comforted her, reminding her that she had not broken her fast that day and was as hollow as a drum. The very thought of food made her feel sick with hunger. This returning instinct seemed to her a bitter triumph for her body, which she had cowed into accepting death, and which now was resurrected and at once clamored for food.

She was in the state of mind in which the bodily functions seem distasteful. Having faced death, it appeared to her to be abhorrent to reenter ordinary life. Her lungs, her heart, her blood had maintained their existence invisibly, imperceptibly, but those processes that she must notice had been suspended. Now they began again. Hunger, weariness, desire for sleep, intruded into the purity of her renunciation of life. Tears trickled down her face as she considered her position. She had made a supreme effort to escape from shame and had been turned back.

Roger, meanwhile, had gone into the shadowed part of the hut and there stripped off his own wet clothes and put on a yellowed laborer's smock and crumpled leggings which he had found with the blanket.

Sabine, as he came back into the dim circle of candlelight, looked at him and began to laugh, her lips quivering helplessly between tears and amusement.

He stared at her, black brows together, dumbfounded.

"It . . . it . . . is so funny," she gasped. "If anyone should see us like this . . . you in a shepherd's smock and me in a horse blanket. . . ."

Despite the basic heaviness of his mood, his lips twitched responsively, seeing the humor of their situation. Then he saw that her laughter verged on hysteria, and he caught her by the shoulders and shook her.

She stopped laughing, clutching at her blanket, which had fallen down, revealing the smooth whiteness of her shoulders, and her rounded breasts.

She pulled it around her again, and he turned away, releasing her shoulders.

"Why did you try to drown yourself?" he asked harshly.

She was too exhausted to dissemble, and it no longer seemed to matter. "I am going to have a baby," she said flatly.

He nodded. He had suspected as much. Young girls varied very little, but he had thought better of this one. She had seemed a sensible, level-headed child. He looked at her with dislike. She was lovely in her disarray, her honey-colored hair streaked dark with water, and her eyes reddened with tears.

"Who is the father?" he demanded.

She looked away, shivering. "No. I cannot tell you that."

"You were with my sister when she eloped," he said in the same rough voice. "When did you leave her? And why?"

"The day after the wedding," she whispered. "I wanted to come home."

"Home? Where is your home?"

She sighed and drew the blanket closer. "I mean to Dorset. My father is in Yorkshire now, and I have no home to go to—but I wanted to come back to Dorset."

"To your lover? He is a Dorset man?" He watched her closely. "Someone here at Ceorlbury, I suppose?"

"No," she said, shaking her head with such firmness that he believed her.

"Who, then?" he pressed.

She did not answer. He watched her, wondering what went on behind the smooth brow and sad blue-green eyes. A sudden suspicion shot through him, and his eyes narrowed.

"It is that scoundrel who married my sister! He seduced you!"

She looked up, stung into indignation. "No, sir, it is not Captain Huntley. He was very kind and generous to me, and I respect him. He never said a word to me that any other living soul could not hear!"

He was forced to accept her word for that and tried to come at the truth another way. After a pause he asked, "When is the child due? You do not show yet."

She flushed. "I . . . I am not sure, sir. I cannot tell. My mother died when I was so young, and I never learnt the signs of it."

"But you are sure you are to have a child?" he asked, a pity for her rising in him at her confused and embarrassed stammering.

She nodded. "I am as certain as I can be, sir."

"When did you begin to think so, then?" he pressed.

"A few days ago, but I should have realized a month since had I been less foolish. I did not understand the signs until I began to feel sick in the mornings."

"So you are only two months pregnant?" he decided.

She considered. "Yes, sir, about that it must be. . . ."

He stood over her, arms folded. "Then it is my cousin, Falcon, who is responsible!"

She saw then how he had come at the truth

by this roundabout fashion and bit her lip, not knowing how to answer.

"Oh, do not bother to deny or admit it," he said roughly. "I read the truth in your face!"

Falcon's indifference to Ceorlbury and Bella Amhurst's elopement had passed through this man's brain like a red-hot poker through muslin, leaving a smoldering trail of anger and hatred. He looked at this girl, so young to be seduced and abandoned in a strange city, and his anger rose fierily in him again. Falcon's behavior towards her merely underlined Roger's assessment of his general character.

The realization that this girl carried Falcon's child struck him forcefully. If Falcon had married her, she might be the mother of the next heir to Ceorlbury.

She was frightened and puzzled by the strangeness of his expression. What was he thinking? She bent her head in shame, feeling that he must be despising her, and wove her fingers into a tent like a child caught out in wrongdoing.

"My cousin never spoke of marriage, of course?" he asked in a dry tone.

Without looking up, she shook her head.

"You have no relative who might take you in until the child is born?"

"None," she said huskily. "My father is my only living relative, and he is so far away. I do not want to bring shame upon him in his new life."

How unjust, he thought, that Falcon should so casually beget a child when I cannot do so! If it were mine, I would marry the girl with joyful thanksgiving and make her mistress of Ceorlbury despite her low birth.

He stared at her, in the dim, flickering candle-light, barely seeing her for the turmoil of his thoughts.

She bore within her his cousin's child, an Amhurst in nature if not in legal title. Flesh of his flesh just as much as if it were to be born in wedlock.

Here, then, was an answer to his angry desire for another heir. If he could not get a son himself, he could pretend to have done so. It would be an ironic retort to Falcon's lustful selfishness and Bella's folly.

Aloud, he said in a solemn tone, "Your child shall have a father. I shall marry you myself."

She stared up at him, her face pallid and dazed. Her brain did not comprehend what he had said, and he had to repeat it many times before she understood.

"But why?" she asked, naturally enough.

"I have no child," he said. "And my family owes you recompense. Your child shall be known as my child. No one shall lose by it. He shall only have his father's inheritance as he ought." And he smiled, oddly.

"He knows," she stammered, "Falcon knows about it . . ."

He looked sharply at her. "You told him you were pregnant?"

"No," she said quickly. "I have not seen him since that night. He went away next morning before I was awake. But he will guess. He will suspect. . . ."

"I hope he does," said Roger, smiling darkly. "He can prove nothing, can he? Let the irony of it eat into his heart—he said he did not want Ceorlbury. He shall not have it. And if he suspects that he was the instrument of his own disinheritance, then so much the better."

She stayed in the hut until dawn when he came for her, dressed in his best clothes, and drove her into Weymouth, where she was given into the care of one of his old servants who kept a lodging house on the front there.

Roger was determined that no shadow should be cast upon his marriage. He had the banns called in the parish of Ceorlbury and ordered a splendid wedding feast for all the tenants in one of his barns.

The servants buzzed with incredulous amazement when they discovered the name of his bride-to-be, and Jabez Starling was able to drink freely for days in recompense for his knowledge of the bride.

"I heard her singing to squire once, all alone in his room. 'Twas her voice first captured him," Jabez said, twirling his empty tankard with a finger.

It was refilled, and he went on, lowering his voice, "I don't say she isn't a modest little creature, but. . . ."

"What a rise in the world for a maid," the gossips sighed, " 'Tis like a story from the Bible, the beggar maid and the king. Why, she will be one of the first ladies in Dorset now, with jewels and gowns and her own carriage!"

The local gentry were not so enthusiastic, however, and letters were hastily sent to Falcon Amhurst in London, but, as he was out of the country, they were left to lie on his desk until his return. His mother and sister were in Bath visiting a sick friend, and by some mischance no news of the marriage reached them there, although they only by one day missed one who could have informed them.

One or two old acquaintances, braver than they knew, called upon Roger Amhurst to attempt to dissuade him from what they called his folly. He was calm and sober and quite undeterred. They even suspected an unexplainable glint in his eye from time to time, as though he laughed at them.

Had they known of her whereabouts, they would have sent their formidable wives to bully Sabine out of the match, but Roger gave no indication as to where she was staying, despite their thinly disguised attempts to discover it.

Sabine arrived from Weymouth with her husband-to-be on the night before the wedding. She went straight to her room, now one of the better bedchambers, and was not seen again until the wedding morning.

During the three weeks which had lapsed, she had, at Roger's insistence, bought a large number of clothes, and the maids were ecstatic over her trousseau.

The wedding day dawned bright and clear for

autumn. The sky was cloudless, the wind soft, and the sun hot upon the heads of the wedding guests as they assembled at the church.

Roger arrived first and paused before going in to look with a strange grin at the tombs of his ancestors, the latest of whom were buried in the churchyard, while the earlier ones had been interred within the church.

Sabine followed soon after, almost unrecognizable in her silk and lace, and the crowded congregation breathed a sigh of involuntary pleasure at her glowing beauty.

"She looks a proper lady," whispered one to Jabez. "Every inch of her."

"I never saw such a change in anyone," he said half-sadly, for beneath the rich costume, he saw vaguely the simple country girl he had met in Dorchester so short a time ago. "We never know what's to come to us, do we? And best we do not, I say."

Jabez gave her away, at her own request, and the squire had fitted him out with new clothes at his expense for the occasion, so that the bailiff felt an even deeper personal interest in the marriage, as one standing in lieu of a father.

Roger Amhurst had written to Sabine's real father for his permission for the marriage and received a curt letter in reply giving it, but refusing to attend. "My child will be best without reminders of her real station in life," wrote Daniel Mudeford. "But," he went on, "her grandfather was a wealthy farmer of some standing in society, so you do not get so poor a bargain as you might imagine."

Roger, conscious of the gossip, allowed this fact to be made generally known, to disarm some of the criticism. It was then decided that Sabine's air of calm serenity in her new station must be laid at the door of ancestry. Her farmer-grandfather became, by some strange transmutation, a gentleman born, and she written down as a natural aristocrat.

Roger had spared no expense for the wedding breakfast. Tables were heaped with food and drink, and every man, woman and child on the estate was invited.

He and Sabine held a smaller party in the house itself for such of the local gentry and the wealthier tenantry who had come, but first they went into the barn to have their healths drunk and accept congratulations before leaving the merry guests to enjoy themselves without let or hindrance.

Sabine smiled and accepted good wishes with poise and grace, her hand upon her new husband's arm where he had placed it. "To the manner born," the people whispered, watching them curiously. "It must be true that her family were gentry once. Else, where would she learn to act so fine?"

The later party was more restrained and less good natured. The time seemed to Sabine to drag past until at last Roger rose and led her to the stairs to change for their coming journey.

They were to visit France, Switzerland and Italy

on their bridal tour. Roger intended to stay abroad for at least a year so that Sabine's child could be born out of the country, thus silencing any gossip over the advanced date of the birth.

When she came down again in her new travelling clothes, she found the estate people waiting outside the house, clustered around the carriage. A bawdy cheer went up, and rice was thrown at them with great enjoyment. Sabine, in a green check travelling dress and cape, with a feathered bonnet, waved as the carriage drew away and threw her bridal bouquet at one of the nicer maids.

When she sat down again, sighing, Roger Amhurst looked at her with concern. "You are very pale. Are you well? You must take care of yourself, you know, for the child's sake."

She smiled shyly. "I am tired and excited, sir."

"Roger," he reminded, frowning.

She blushed. "Roger," she whispered, looking away. She was not yet accustomed to the idea of marriage to him and was not sure how to behave. While they were in public, she had acted out a part, but now she was stiff and uneasy.

He leaned back, closing his eyes. "Get some sleep, then," he ordered curtly. "We have a long journey ahead of us."

Two days later, Falcon Amhurst rode up to Ceorlbury and stumbled over the threshold, demanding to see his cousin.

When he was informed by a curious and excited butler that the wedding had been celebrated and the bridal pair gone two days on their tour, he stared, going white, then without a word turned on his heel and left again.

"Somebody's nose is right out of joint," remarked a maid under her breath.

"Poor young gentleman," sighed a more romantic friend. "So handsome, and now he is cheated of his inheritance. He will not have the house now."

"It don't necessarily follow," the butler remarked in stately condescension. "Marriage is one thing. Children is another. Master was married before and no sign of an heir."

A serving man grinned coarsely. "Ah, but gentry don't marry beneath 'em for no good reason. Mark my words, Squire knew he had a loaf in the oven afore he ever thought to open the door."

The maids shrieked with laughter, and the butler frowned. "I don't want such talk here. Hold your silly tongues."

The serving man, unrepentant, said, "I don't blame Squire. A bird in the hand is worth two in the bush. And that first wife of his was as plain as a barn door, while this one is a pretty armful of joy."

"Squire never even touched the girl," said Jabez Starling, suddenly appearing with a frown.

"That wasn't your story last week," they reminded him.

"I was drunk," he retorted. "You saw her on her wedding day. Did she look to you the sort of girl who would let herself be taken lightly, eh?"

"All I know is that Squire wanted an heir des-

perate bad," said the serving man. "He hated
Master Falcon like rat poison. And I hope the girl
is in the family way. This old house needs a family
in it, I say!"

Falcon Amhurst, riding into Dorchester to find
a bed for the night, was driven by thoughts too
dark for any of the servants to comprehend.

He had been ashamed of himself on the morning after he seduced Sabine. His heartfelt shame
had made him leave at once to give him time to
consider how to deal with the situation. When he
went back two days later, it was to find the
Huntleys gone from their lodgings.

"To France," the lodging-house keeper had
said, and when he asked if the maid had been
with them, she had shrugged and said she supposed so, but could not say.

Falcon had followed and at length tracked
down the bridal pair in Paris. There Philip Huntley reproachfully informed him of Sabine's flight
back to Dorchester.

"Do you think she went to Ceorlbury, Philip?"
he had asked anxiously.

"She said she could not return there," Philip
said, and asked with a frown what he intended
to do. "You cannot marry a common serving
wench, Falcon."

Falcon plunged his head into his hands. "How
can I know until I have seen her? I can think of
nothing else. I am consumed with anxiety for
her, Philip. She was such a lovely little creature,
so sweet and gentle. I have wronged her so badly.
I must do what I can to recompense her."

"Money, you mean?" Philip asked with undisguised contempt. "She would not take it from you."

"I do not know what I mean," he cried angrily. "I feel impelled to find her, though."

"You can only harm her further. Let her forget you."

"But she may be in trouble," Falcon said miserably. "She may need my help."

"If she is bearing your child?" Philip sighed. "That had not occurred to me. But wait a while, and we will see if we can find her when we get back to England. Stay with us for a few days, Falcon. I've missed you. Bella's company can be wearisome when she is in a bad mood."

Falcon laughed at his friend's dispirited air. "Is she a bore? But, she is rich, Philip. Comfort yourself with that."

Philip looked seriously at him. "I would have done better to find some honest employment. She nags me ragged."

Bella, when she discovered that Falcon had arrived, added her pleadings to her husband's, and Falcon agreed to remain there for a while.

When they returned to England together, they were busy for a while in finding a house for the newlyweds to rent in London. Bella had no intention of wasting herself in the country again and employed her time happily in organizing her new household. Falcon was therefore already too late when he at last opened the letter bringing the news of Roger's marriage. Philip, who was with him, was sipping a glass of wine and idly swinging his polished boots in a shaft of sunlight when he heard Falcon emit a groan.

Looking up, he found his friend white to the lips, holding a letter in a hand that shook.

"What is it, man?" He grabbed his shoulder in concern. "You look quite ill. Is it bad news?"

Wordlessly, Falcon held out the letter.

Philip took it, frowning into his friend's face, then read it and pursed his lips in a whistle of amazement.

"Good God! Can it be true?"

"What reason could there be to invent such a tale?" said Falcon dryly. "I must go down there at once and stop the marriage."

Philip nodded. "I would not have thought it of that girl. She had such honest eyes. Yet she must have tricked your cousin into this marriage. It is incredible that he should ever have consented to it, but when once he knows that she has been your mistress, he will be shocked and angry."

"I do not give a damn for Roger," Falcon said between clenched teeth. "But she is mine . . . I cannot let another man have her!"

Philip was shocked and stared at him. "Falcon! My God, man, what are you saying?"

"That I love her," Falcon groaned. "I was blind not to know it before. Oh, if I had only come back from France at once. If I had not run off that morning, but had stayed and married her . . ."

"You cannot marry her," Philip said incredulously. "You will be ruined! Neither of you will be invited anywhere. You will be ostracized."

"What the devil do I care for that, you fool?" snapped Falcon, stalking from the room.

He had ridden to Ceorlbury as though the devil rode behind him, but he had come too late, and, as he made his way to Dorchester, he ached for some action which might relieve the bitter pressure on his emotions. Had he met Roger then, he would have killed him without hesitation. The violence of his expression made the innkeeper stare at him dubiously, but he demanded brandy in a tone which admitted of no refusal, and the man scurried to obey. He drank without pause until he fell forward on the table, dead drunk, his last conscious thought a passionate prayer for revenge upon Sabine and her new husband.

CHAPTER FOUR

A YEAR had passed before Sabine and Roger Amhurst came home again to England. Jabez Starling governed the estate at Ceorlbury with devoted loyalty, writing once a month to his absent master with all the news he thought necessary for him to hear. From time to time he had a brief reply, always dated from some new city, scribbled hastily in the intervals of sight-seeing and pleasure, yet conveying to Jabez, who knew him so well, a certain note of homesickness.

Roger did not tell Jabez anything of what he and Sabine did on their travels, although there was much he could have told which would have interested everyone at Ceorlbury.

The time was well spent in those foreign cities. Roger paid through the nose to have Sabine's manners polished, her knowledge of etiquette carefully instilled, her accent refined down to a pleasantly articulated burr so that she did not quite lose her Dorset tones but was not quite so plainly of the people. Roger himself spoke in two tongues: that of the Ceorlbury tenants, the Dorset murmur, and that of his own class, a more incisive clipping of words. He preferred the former, but he knew that Sabine must be able to carry off social occasions with an accent acceptable to the gentry. Her birth might one day be forgiven her, but only if she could contrive to bury it under an acquired gentility.

She loved Italy, finding the dark-skinned, voluble friendly people easy to like, and as her body thickened, so their gentleness increased. Maternity was held in awe there, and her servants treated her as though she were made of fragile china.

Her child was born in a small villa in the warm south on a bright March morning. The birth was not easy, but she had the loving sympathy of some half-dozen Italian matrons to support her, and as it was a saint's day, there was a constant ringing of bells outside the villa from the three local churches.

The midwife delivered the child, laughing. *"Bambino,"* she cried in triumph. *"Bambino, signora. . . ."*

Dazed and sleepy, Sabine leaned forward and sighed as she saw her son being lovingly handled by the women.

When the child was slapped and oiled and wrapped in the swaddling robes, Sabine was made comfortable on piled pillows before her husband was admitted.

He came in haltingly, very pale and nervous. Now that the event had actually arrived he was afraid that the child would be a girl, and thus defeat the purpose of his marriage. But the beaming dark faces soon reassured him, and his joy delighted them as he frankly wept and embraced them with what, in an Englishman, was considered remarkably sensible behavior.

"Bambino," they congratulated him, kissing his cheeks, and he as uninhibitedly kissed them back, crying, "A son, a son," with wet eyes.

They pushed him, laughing, at his wife, and he kissed her reverently upon the forehead and then again upon her hands.

"Ah . . ." breathed the women from the door. "Bella. . . ."

It was, they agreed, as they left with tactful sympathy, a lovely sight. The husband so dark. Almost Italian, they nodded. And the wife so young and blonde and lovely. How happy they had been with their new son. That was how it should be—and they asked each other was it possible that the stories of frigid Englishmen and women were all false? Such emotional joy at the birth of a first son was typically Italian, but it was surprising in an Englishman.

Left alone together, the husband and wife soon lapsed into a difficult silence. Roger's first overwhelming joy subsided a little, and he sat down upon the chair beside the bed, clearing his throat with embarrassment. He had never wept in public before. It was these damned foreigners with their queer ways. He had been away from home too long.

Good God, he thought angrily, the boy isn't even mine!

Then his glance fell upon the carved wooden cradle in which the child slept curled up like a tiny puppy, one small hand on his cheek.

A strange tenderness twisted his heavy face into

a smile. "Is he well made?" he asked Sabine in sudden anxiety. "He looks very small."

"He is perfect," she breathed. She was not yet used to being treated as his equal, and now and then almost found herself calling him sir. She wondered what he was thinking behind that dark mask of his which so much reminded her of Falcon. They had the same heavy brows, the same black hair, the same shaped mouth. Only their cast of features was different, Roger having a heavy, brooding look, while Falcon was clean-cut and chiselled.

He had never treated her with intimacy. Their marriage remained unconsummated. She knew intuitively that while she bore another man's child, he would never regard her as his wife, but now that the child was born, their marriage proper might also begin.

Theirs was an unstable and delicate relationship founded upon a lie, and she was uneasy about the future. She had given him the son he needed, and she saw that he was grateful and happy, but what would be their future relationship?

He turned from his deep contemplation of the child and smiled at her. "An heir for Ceorlbury," he said, a grim note of satisfaction in his voice. "I shall always treat the boy as my son, my dear. You need have no fear on that score." His eyes moved back to the cradle. "Do you think he has the Amhurst face?" he asked in an oddly wistful tone. "I may be imagining it, but he seems to me to be a perfect Amhurst."

She leaned over and studied the tiny face with

a smile. "He does have your nose," she said in surprise. "Yes, he does."

Roger flushed. "I thought that!" he said delightedly. "It looks damned odd on that small face." He glanced apologetically at her. "Sorry, my dear. I forgot my language."

She smiled. On an impulse, she held out her hand to him. "You will love him, Roger?" she asked, using his name for the first time in private.

He took the hand between both of his and bent his head to kiss her fingers. "I will," he promised. "I mean to bring him up as my son, you know. He shall have Ceorlbury, and I will teach him to love the place as I do." Privately he thought that the boy should never grow up as his real father had, despising the land on which all his wealth was based. He should live on the estate and only go away to school. He must be trained to regard Ceorlbury as the only place in the world where one could be happy.

He kissed Sabine again, and went away to celebrate the birth with those of the English colony whom he had met.

Sabine lay gazing at the mild, blue sky beyond her window. The future seemed to her troubled and uncertain despite what Roger had said. Since her marriage, she had had no time for reflection. So much had happened to her. Now, looking back, she wondered if she had been wise to marry Roger. She might have leapt out of the frying pan into the fire.

The child stirred, opening his eyes, and she

caught her breath. They were the same blue, the same shape as Falcon Amhurst's.

To the noisy regret of their servants, they moved on from the little whitewashed villa a month later and began to make their way slowly back across Europe. Sabine had now recovered her figure, and Roger insisted on calling in a bevy of dressmakers to make her a new wardrobe before they set off so that their luggage grew heavier at every stop as he generously bought her hats, gloves, hose, underwear, lace and ribbons galore. She was half-frightened by the tide of gifts which poured from him, but his very obvious delight and pride in her renewed beauty forced her to accept his gifts with a show of gratitude.

He kept up her lessons, too, reading aloud with her to improve her accent, watching as Italian or French dancing masters demonstrated the latest steps to her, nodding and smiling as she fumbled her way through an easy piece of music before launching, with a sigh of relief, into a song.

"Madame has a very pretty singing voice," one French music master told him admiringly. "The sweetest I ever trained. If you stayed here two years, I could make her voice really remarkable. It needs to be disciplined."

But Roger shook his head. "It is very well as nature intended it," he said firmly, "but she must learn to play the piano well enough to be heard in our home. Concentrate on the piano, m'sieur."

The Frenchman sighed. "She is too old to learn correctly, I am afraid. Her fingering is stiff." But he obeyed, and Sabine in fact learned to play quite simple little tunes well enough.

The baby, Guy, named for Roger's father, grew daily more like an Amhurst. He was small and slight in build, but his hair was a black thatch before he was three months, and everyone who saw him commented upon that Amhurst nose. "So like his father," cooed an exiled English lady whom they met in Poitiers.

Roger's heavy face became dark red, and he cleared his throat roughly without speaking.

So successful had Sabine's tutors been that those of their countrymen whom they met hardly seemed to notice that she was not of the same status as her husband. She learned to mix with her husband's acquaintances as naturally as though she had always been used to such company, and as familiarity bred ease with her, she soon left off blushing and feeling shy with well-bred strangers.

They took the whole of the summer to make their way home. Roger had announced the birth of his son to his relatives by letter some weeks after the birth, being careful to give no date for the birth. He wanted no slur to be cast upon his son's name, and the later that birth was supposed to have taken place the better. He knew well enough that uncharitable voices would whisper that he had married the girl because he had got her with child already, but the less proof of such suspicion the better.

When his letter reached a certain tall house in London, the recipient, Julia Amhurst, stiffened over her breakfast table, glared at the offending epistle, crunched it into a ball and flung it at the wall. For a moment she sat staring at nothing, then she rang her bell violently and, when a panting servant appeared, sent for her son and daughter in a tone which carried throughout the house.

Falcon, wrapped in a silk dressing gown, strolled along the corridor. He leaned against the door, one brow raised.

"My dear Mama, must you disturb my sleep so early?"

His sister threw him a warning glance over her shoulder. She was leaning over her mother, a glass bottle of sal volatile in her hand.

"It is all your fault," moaned his mother. "To throw away your future so carelessly by offending Roger! You have ruined yourself now!"

His glanced sharpened. "What now?"

"She has had a son!" his mother snapped, pointing at the letter which still lay on the floor where she had thrown it.

He straightened, the mocking smile gone from his eyes, and crossed to pick it up. Smoothing it out, he read the letter slowly. "It does not say when the child was born," he said aloud to himself.

"And for a very good reason," his mother said bitterly. "I do not doubt, and I did not doubt at the time he married her, that he had got her into trouble. Why else should he marry a servant? You may depend upon it, she's no better than she should be! She was probably six months gone before the marriage ceremony!"

"It is so humiliating," Fanny said. "How could

cousin Roger marry one of his servants? Everyone in London is always laughing at me behind my back. They all know the story. It is the scandal of the century."

"Do not talk such arrant nonsense, Fanny," said Falcon with irritable weariness. "You imagine things. We are not important enough to be so interesting."

"What do you mean to do about it, Falcon?" asked his mother. "You see, he has the impudence to write that we will all be invited to Ceorlbury for his child's christening! We shall not go, of course."

He turned his head slowly and looked at her with a bitter smile, "Oh, yes, Mama, we will!"

"What?" she cried in amazement.

"I refuse to go," said Fanny, tossing her head. "Go down there to be patronized by a common servant girl? Not I!"

Her brother's lips parted from each other in a dangerous grin. "You will do as you are told, Fanny," he said with complete conviction, and she backed away from him in alarm. She had never seen her brother look with such ferocity. It reminded her of the caged panther she had once seen, snarling silently and impotently at her through iron bars.

He looked at his mother, his brows raised. "We will all go," he said flatly, and turned on his heel and left.

Mrs. Amhurst looked in silence at Fanny for a long moment, her mouth open and rounded. Then she said, "Well . . ." on a long sigh.

"What can he mean?" Fanny asked quiveringly. "I do not understand him."

"He is the most selfish, foolish fellow who ever lived," said Mrs. Amhurst crossly. "Why did he ever encourage that silly Arabella to run off with Philip Huntley in the first place? He must have known how it would anger Roger. And although there is no sign of a child there, anyone could have foreseen that a child might result. Is he mad to throw the estate away in such a scapegrace fashion?"

"I do not know why cousin Roger disapproved of Philip," said Fanny, softly smiling. "He is far too good for Bella, if the truth were told! She is a spiteful, sharp-tongued harpy! I am sorry for Philip. He bears with her so gently."

Mrs. Amhurst eyed her suspiciously, "You visit them too often, Fanny. I do not like this intimacy which has grown up between you and that man Huntley!"

"Oh, Mama," said Fanny, flushing bright red and leaping to her feet. "Really! Intimacy!"

"Friendship, then—call it what you will! It is dangerous for your good name to see so much of him."

"Bella is always there," she protested, still very red. "And I am not likely to forget that Philip is her husband. She makes her claims upon him very clear to every female he meets."

The bitterness of Fanny's tone escaped her mother, who merely repeated, "See a little less of them, all the same." Then, reverting to their previous topic with barely a pause, "Oh, I could murder Falcon! He seems to have deliberately wrecked his chance of inheriting Ceorlbury. Anyone would think he disliked the place."

"So he does," said Fanny flatly.

Her mother ignored her. "Money is all very well, but land is what makes a gentleman. The prospect seemed so bright last year when Roger invited us down there. And yet now Falcon is cut out by a mere servant girl and her brat. If he had only taken the trouble to please Roger! But he will always go his own way. He is so selfish!"

"He could always buy himself an estate," Fanny pointed out a little dryly. "He has enough money to buy another Ceorlbury and still be considered very wealthy."

Mrs. Amhurst sniffed. "You cannot buy the standing which inheriting Ceorlbury would have given him. The Amhursts have lived there for centuries. Any upstart can buy land. But that does not mean anything." She looked at Fanny thoughtfully, "Do you expect Sir George Shirley today? Such a pleasant man."

Fanny looked rebellious. "Mama, I do not like him! He has hairy hands."

"Good heavens, child, as if that matters! He has a castle in Northumberland and a considerable fortune. What would it matter if he had six hands and three heads? I think him an excellent match for you."

Fanny wordlessly retreated and very soon was hurrying round to the house which Bella had taken on lease. Philip Huntley met her in the drawing room, his fair face lighting up as she entered. Fanny's own lips quivered as he lightly touched her hand in greeting.

"Has Bella heard the news?" she asked with a determined smile.

There was the sound of shattering china from upstairs, and Philip's eyes met Fanny's.

"Yes," he said. "Yes, she has heard."

Fanny could hardly control her desire to comfort him and, clenching her hands at her side, said, "I will go up to her."

Philip sighed. "Thank you, Fanny," he said.

The attachment which had sprung up between these two was the stronger for being undeclared and firmly controlled. They had known each other for years, but it was only when Philip was her cousin's husband that Fanny began to feel more than common interest in him. She was, of course, aware of his reasons for marrying Bella, and perhaps aware that had she herself shown response to him earlier, he might have married her. She felt no scorn for his actions. A marriage of convenience was too common to arouse anything but the faintest curiosity. She had first felt pity for him, seeing his wife's treatment of him, and then admiration for his restraint in reply and his public displays of contentment which she knew must be assumed.

When she entered Bella's chamber, it was to find her sitting at her dressing table with the pieces of a china powder bowl around her feet.

Bella swung round, lips spitting fury. "That little slut has had a brat!" she screamed. "When I think that I brought her into the family. I encouraged her to have ideas above her station. If I had her here now I would pull every hair from her head!"

Fanny stayed with her for some time, soothing her as much as she could, for Philip's sake.

When she left her, Bella had returned to bed and was moaning that she had a headache and would sleep for an hour or two.

In the drawing room, Fanny found Philip talking to Falcon. As she entered, she heard her brother, in a voice so filled with anguish that she did not know it, say, "I am suffering the tortures of the damned, Philip."

She stared at him, and both men swung round, an awkward silence falling.

"Falcon, what is the matter?" she asked anxiously. "Are you ill?"

He grinned easily, "Toothache, my dear Fanny, that is all, but it has kept me awake half the night."

"Have you taken oil of cloves? Why did you say nothing to Mama this morning?"

He shrugged. "She would only fuss over me. I shall live. How is Bella?"

She glanced uneasily at Philip. "She is sleeping."

He looked relieved. "She does not want me to go up?"

"I do not think so," Fanny told him reassuringly.

Falcon watched them, a small frown pleating his brows as a new thought occurred to him.

He had come here to see Philip alone, to discuss the birth of Sabine's child with him. His first thought on reading the letter bearing the news had been to suspect the child as his own. The omission of the child's date of birth seemed proof enough to him, but then he had wondered if Sabine had been the innocent she had appeared. Had Roger been her lover before ever he met her? Had she been secretly laughing at him with her air of modest shyness? How much of that gentle virtue had been a mask?

His jealousy, given soil to breed in, had multiplied rapidly into a tortured certainty that Sabine had made a fool of him. She must have meant all along to be mistress of Ceorlbury and had encouraged him in order to have both cousins on a string. Well, she had been clever, he told himself. She was married to Roger and had borne him a son. Had her marriage been childless, she must have feared Roger's death and his succession. Now she need fear no one. But still the question tortured him—whose child was it? His or his cousin's?

Fanny had spoken to him twice before he looked up. She smiled, puzzled and anxious, "I was asking if you were seriously intending to go to Ceorlbury for that christening?"

His head lifted, a strange smile stealing round the corners of his mouth. "Oh, yes," he said slowly, "I would not miss it for anything, Fanny."

She shrank back in alarm at the bitterness of his blue eyes. Sometimes she was positively frightened of him. His moods grew more odd and contrary day by day.

"Will you walk back with me, Falcon?" she asked nervously, "I must get back before Mama misses me."

He shook his head. "I have matters to discuss with Philip," he answered evasively.

At the first hint of autumn, Roger grew restless. "I am tired of France," he told Sabine. "Shall we go home?"

She agreed willingly, aware that he longed to be home for the opening of the hunting season. They packed up and set off for the coast a week later, and within three days were on the Dorchester road to Ceorlbury. Sabine was very nervous about facing the servants at the house, but Roger was so accustomed to her company that he had almost forgotten that she had once been his servant. His whole mind was concentrated on reaching his home. He longed to sleep once more within his own walls, hear the night cry of owl or fox, smell the fresh damp scent of the grass in the mornings when he rode out at dawn through woods of russet and gold where blue mists stole at ground level until the sun came up, and cobwebs adorned the undergrowth, glittering with dew.

Italy had been beautiful, but the bold colors and hot suns were wearying to English eyes, and as he stared hungrily about him, he rejoiced in the multihued landscape spreading on every side, green melting into rust, gold into bronze, the roads awash with crisp leaves, and the trees stripping for winter.

Their arrival at Ceorlbury was attended by half the tenantry. Noisily expressing their joy in the new heir, they pressed around the carriage, throwing up their hats and cheering. The servants had lined up on the steps to welcome them home, but Sabine was so overwhelmed by the loud greetings of the tenants that she passed this obstacle with hardly a faltering of her step.

Roger had determined on an early christening. The invitations were sent out, and the house became a hive of industry. The old christening robe was brought down from the attics, washed with loving care and given new ribbons. The unused rooms were thrown open, stripped, scrubbed and made ready for new occupants. The kitchen became frantic with energy.

Sabine's new poise and beauty was the talk of the district. She had come back to Ceorlbury in an elegant blue silk gown trimmed with French lace, the skirt very full, the bodice tight and close-fitting at the neck. The very latest fashion, the servants agreed. And she looked quite the lady, her honey-color hair dressed in soft curls that fell to her ears and cascaded down her back.

She had brought back with her from France a personal maid of ripe years called Marette, a swarthy, stolid, businesslike woman with big brown eyes, firm lips and a reticence which soon made her feared but respected among the other servants. Marette silently adored her mistress, who had been kind to her, and made for Sabine a barrier between herself and the household. Marette's devotion to the new lady of Ceorlbury made it easier for Sabine to take up the reins of command in the house.

She began quietly by asking the housekeeper

to bring her the account books and went on in the same gentle, firm fashion, leaving no opening for insolence or disobedience to flourish. The servants' gossip died down. They shrugged and accepted that a new era had begun at Ceorlbury.

One could not take liberties with someone who looked so much like one of the gentry, whose voice and manner exactly fitted her position. Had Sabine come back speaking the Dorset dialect, wearing her simple clothes, or acting in the same shy fashion, they might have treated her with contempt. But she was no longer the same girl, and in the year that had passed since her marriage, the servants had lost their first incredulous scorn of their master's marriage and grown accustomed to the fact.

Roger, nevertheless, waited impatiently for the replies to his invitations. He wanted Sabine to be accepted by his own world. She was the mother of the future master of Ceorlbury and must be received by the county families.

Many were the discussions held in houses all over Dorset. "Such misalliances bring fresh blood into old families," stated Lady Carlew to her three indignant sons. "The Amhursts have always been eccentric anyway. I shall go. Whether you do or not is entirely your own affair."

Her eldest son, the master of Carlew Manor, Sir George, threw back his rather thin shoulders and looked down his long nose. "Unwise of you, Mama. Amhurst must be insane to marry one of his servants. Unheard-of scandal. Do we even have any assurance that the child is his? Eh? Eh?"

His brothers, the twins James and John, mumbled agreement, their expressions divided between apprehension of their terrifying mother and a wish to please their elder brother upon whose bounty they relied for their income.

Lady Carlew snorted. "Silly damned fool, George. What difference does it make? Legally, the boy's his heir. We'll have to know the boy sooner or later. Can't cut the Amhursts off entirely. Why antagonize the girl now? You'll only leave her free to fill the child's head with odd notions." She drew herself up to her full five foot one. "I shall take the chit in hand. Teach her the right things to do. She's an Amhurst now, like it or not. We must put up with it."

Her sons continued to protest for days, but they knew in their hearts that the maternal edict would stand. And in many other homes much the same decision was made. The new Lady of Ceorlbury might be beneath notice, but her son would be too important for them to ignore.

When Mrs. Amhurst wrote from London, accepting the invitation on behalf of herself and her two children, Roger stared at the letter for a long time before he passed it silently to Sabine.

She read it and looked at him, eyes wide. "He . . . he is coming, then," she murmured, holding her voice level by a great effort.

"It seems so," said Roger roughly.

She swallowed. "And . . . if he makes a scene? Says something?"

"He is a scoundrel," said Roger, raising a dark brow. "But he is a gentleman. He'll say nothing."

She was not convinced. She dreaded seeing Falcon again. Her brief love affair had had such a tragic result and had nearly ended in her death. She could not forgive him, and at the same time she feared the powerful attraction he held for her. He must suspect Guy to be his own son and surely must be angry at seeing the child supplant him. But what would he do?

Her year abroad had taught her to control her outward expression however, and no one seeing her welcoming her guests to the christening a week later could have suspected that she was inwardly tortured with suspense.

Her beauty and air of breeding surprised those who had come to sneer at a common country girl, reminding them of the rumors that she was of good descent a generation or two back. They were sufficiently surprised to react with automatic courtesy to her greeting. Watching them, Roger was amused and pleased. He had married her on an impulse of revenge. He was growing proud of her as each month passed.

Under her calmness, though, she was as taut as a bowstring, waiting for Falcon to arrive.

When she saw him arrive, she felt a violent shock run through her, her nerves jerking as though in contact with fire. But she came forward, smilingly, her hand outstretched, as though he were just another guest.

The guests in the background fell silent, watching with close attention this meeting between the deposed heir and his usurping enemy.

Roger turned his head, eyes watchful, but allowed her to be the first to welcome him.

There was cool derision in Falcon's blue eyes as he took the hand she held out and lifted it to his lips. His eyes remained fixed on her face, which only he could see, and as his mouth touched her fingers, he saw her wince, heard a tiny intake of breath and felt her quiver.

He straightened, looking down into her face with that old, intimate, secret smile. "You are a constant amazement to me," he murmured beneath his breath. "I had supposed it impossible for you to increase in beauty, yet you have managed it. Foreign travel has doubled your loveliness." His tone was lazy, warm, as though nothing of what had happened had ever been, and she was almost dumb with confusion and surprise.

She could almost have believed the past to have been a dream, the figment of her imagination, except for the living, breathing fact which lay in its cradle upstairs.

While she was still stricken dumb with confused anger, Falcon looked past her at his cousin, his brows lifted quizzically, the derisive smile lingering on his mouth. From Roger's darkened face and narrowed, angry eyes, he guessed that his cousin knew a great deal more about the relations between his wife and his erstwhile heir than he had suspected.

"My dear Roger," he drawled, "I must congratulate you on your wife. She is even more enchanting than when I last saw her." His own jealousy and hurt made the words dagger-sharp, intended to wound, and he had the satisfaction of seeing them strike home.

Roger's lips drew back from his teeth in a snarl, and he stepped forward without thinking, massive head held at an aggressive angle, shoulders hunched.

Sabine's heart leapt into her mouth. This was what she had feared. Falcon had come determined to cause trouble.

CHAPTER FIVE

SHE quickly went to Roger's side and took his hand firmly. "You are too kind," she said aloud to Falcon, and added to her husband, "Come and bid your sister welcome, my love."

Roger blinked as though dragged from some trance, but he obeyed her in a childlike way as she led him past Falcon towards Bella and her husband who, with Mrs. Amhurst and Fanny, had stood in the background, watching the little scene.

Bella, who had only attended this ceremony in order to put Sabine ruthlessly in her place, was too taken aback by her new sister-in-law's poise and calmness to act out her design. She awkwardly embraced Sabine, touching a cool cheek to hers, and was pleased by the warmth of Sabine's greeting to Philip. Bella had her own reasons for wanting the family rift to be healed. Her elopement, although not regretted, had brought about a certain coldness towards her in society, and it could only do good for Philip to be received by her brother as an accepted member of the family.

Philip's gentle smile brought a faint moisture to Sabine's eyes. They exchanged a brief glance of understanding before she turned to Mrs. Amhurst and Fanny.

Roger scowled incoherently at Philip, kissed

Bella briefly and, like a great sheep dog following a lamb, joined his wife.

Philip took Bella's arm, pressing it. He hoped to keep her thus silenced for the whole of their stay here. He had not been optimistic enough to expect her to behave so well.

Throughout the journey from London, she had expressed her intention of insulting Sabine publicly. "Be received in my own home by my maid! The humiliation! How could Roger be so petty? It was spite made him do it, mark my words! He wished to insult me for having eloped with you! Well, they shall not get away with it!"

Philip had exchanged a wry glance with Falcon now and then, wondering how the other man managed to look so casual about this journey. Only the occasional twitch of a cheek muscle betrayed any inner disturbance.

Bella, like most people, was too absorbed in her own affairs to be capable of believing others might have separate griefs. She gave to her brother the emotions she would have felt in his place, and since spite was one of her governing reactions, she saw in his marriage an act of spite.

She was also becoming anxious because she showed no sign of bearing a child, and Sabine's immediate motherhood irritated and angered her. Jealousy, spite and humiliation ran like poison through her veins. In her rage, she became Mrs. Amhurst's dearest friend, the two women conferring in furtive whispers about their proposed attitude to the new mistress of Ceorlbury. Yet each had separate reasons for feeling a secret triumph over the other: Bella pleased that Mrs. Amhurst's pretensions of seeing her son installed in the estate were totally at an end; and Mrs. Amhurst feeling that Bella had married beneath her and was to be pitied.

Now, as Mrs. Amhurst forced a smile, too cowardly now that the time was here to do as she had intended, Bella whispered to Philip, "Look at her fawning upon them! And yet she patronizes me for having married you, the hypocrite! At least I married a gentleman!"

He patted her arm, flushing. Daily he regretted his marriage and cursed the weakness that had tempted him to it, but never more than now when his wife's nature showed in such cruel clarity.

Sabine held her head high as she and Roger left behind them the little knot of relatives. The worst was over, and somehow a scene of disastrous proportions had been avoided, but she could not relax. She was too conscious of the explosive qualities present in the room.

A short, stout woman caught at her arm suddenly, and she looked round in surprise, meeting a pair of imperious eyes.

"Lady Carlew," murmured Roger in reminder.

Sabine gave a nervous smile.

"I have not seen the view from the terrace for ten years, my dear," Lady Carlew said. "Will you show me?"

Startled but obedient, Sabine took her arm, and they walked through the crowded drawing room and out through the conservatory on to the terrace.

Lady Carlew gazed down the lawns at the walled rose garden. "Ah, yes, very pretty," she dismissed curtly, then looked round at Sabine. "That was just an excuse, of course."

"Oh, indeed?" Sabine was baffled but somehow sensed that this strange, rather awe-inspiring woman meant well by her.

"My family call me the Dowager," said Lady Carlew oddly. "I rather like it. It has a ring, y'know." She stood back and looked Sabine up and down, "You did very well today, m'dear. To the manner born. Is it true you've good blood, or is that one of these romantic taradiddles the people put about?"

"My grandfather was a farmer," said Sabine quietly. "He was quite well to do, but I do not think he had any pretense of gentility."

"Good, good," said the Dowager, looking sidelong at her with bright, interested eyes. "I like the truth. Glad to know you, m'dear. We shall deal very well together. One of my ancestors married a dairymaid. She died without issue, mind you. But she was accepted. These modern young people are too straitlaced for my fancy. Prudery and prisms! Why, Charles II had sons by a little commoner, and nobody looked askance. One of his by-blows almost became king. The world gets smaller every year."

Sabine laughed, suddenly relaxed. "Thank you, Lady Carlew. I am very glad you came today."

The Dowager nodded. "Call me Dowager. Everybody does. Except my sons, and they're all fools. Falcon was acting up, wasn't he?" And she gave Sabine one of her sharp looks.

"He resents me," evaded Sabine.

"Hmm . . . a spoiled boy. His father died when he was still under his mother's thumb, and he has had no firm hand on the reins since. A boy needs a kick now and then to let him know he does not own the world."

Sabine said nothing, and the Dowager gave her another of her penetrating stares.

"You've the quality of silence. I like that in a girl. And firm eyes. Good, good. You handled Falcon and Roger very cleverly—men are like children sometimes." She nodded, "We must go back, now. But I will call on you next week. And you must bring Roger to dinner. He was always a positive hermit. You must not let him slide back into his old ways now, you know."

Arm in arm they went back, and the assembled company watched with deep interest. Lady Carlew was well respected in the county. If she took one of her unaccountable fancies to the new Lady of Ceorlbury, then Sabine's future was settled. Everyone would call. Except those stiff-backed reactionaries who had merely ignored Roger's invitation and would never accept Sabine at any cost. But the majority of the county would follow Lady Carlew's lead.

The ceremony itself was smooth and simple, and afterwards the guests assembled again for the christening feast. Roger was well satisfied with his day. His heir was publicly accepted by society, and the Amhurst family was outwardly reunited.

He had invited Bella at Sabine's pleading. Now he was pleased that he had done so, since she had behaved quite well.

It was as well for his peace of mind that he did not overhear a conversation between Falcon and a depressed gentleman whom he had met by chance for the first time that day.

"I'm ruined, Amhurst," he was saying to Falcon, draining his sixth glass of wine and getting little cheer from it, by his look. "Plucked to the last feather. Shall have to sell up. Thank God I've no son to reproach me. M'wife died last year, poor woman. Glad she didn't live to see it all go, by God."

"Cards?" inquired Falcon sympathetically.

"And women." The man took the new glass Falcon offered him and eyed it with melancholy. "And this! Why does one do it? But there you are—one must do something."

Falcon's smile lingered, but his eyes were suddenly sharp and thoughtful. "Where did you say your land ran?"

"Fratton's Hill," the other replied in surprise. "You must know it, dear fellow—runs along the top of the hill up there." Waving towards the windows. "You can't see the house from down here—back behind the trees. Great barracks of a place, y'know. Falling down around my ears."

Falcon's smile was needle-sharp. "How much do you want for it?"

Suddenly alert, the other asked, "Why? You interested?" And a gleam of intelligence came into the wine-glazed eyes. "Looking for a place of your own now you're out of the running here, eh?"

"Something like that," said Falcon slowly, his eyes resting briefly on the back of Sabine's honey-colored hair.

"Good thing to have your own place," the owner agreed. "See my lawyer if you're serious. Damned fellow has it all in his hands. Hardly cover my debts by selling the place, he says. They are bloodsuckers, those legal fellows. But devilish cunning."

Falcon nodded, "Who is he?"

"Smethers of Smethers, Rundwick and Floy," the other told him. "And watch him, Amhurst—he'll skin you if he can."

Falcon smiled, wryly and with amusement. "He can try. But look here, not a word to a soul until the contracts are signed. I want no rivals in this business."

The other blinked. "Oh, aye. Mum's the word." And, passing out cold a moment or two later, he forgot the whole episode entirely for weeks.

When the majority of the guests had left, the Amhurst family settled down for a few days to a select gathering. It was too far from London for a short visit, and Roger had to stiffen his sinews against irritation with them all. His resentment against Philip died the next day when he overheard him struggling gently against Bella's vituperative outbursts of rage. Roger, who barely knew his sister, was disgusted at her behavior, and a grudging respect for Philip awoke in him.

He intervened with what discretion he could

muster and took Philip off to shoot over the coverts.

"You're a fair shot," he congratulated him later. "Come to the gun room and we'll have a drink together."

Philip looked round the little room with interest and walked about admiring the guns. Roger poured brandy and watched him with curiosity.

"I think I underestimated you, Huntley," he said roughly. "I apologize."

Philip looked round, flushing. "Not at all." He hesitated, then said quickly, "You made a good assessment, in fact." And met Roger's eyes directly, with a slightly wry smile.

"You married Bella for the money?" Roger drained his brandy slowly and set down the glass. "Then I'm sorry for you. You got the worst of the bargain from what I've seen of her. I hardly know her. She was in London mostly. Trying to catch a husband. Cost me a fortune. I should have thanked you for taking her off my hands, but I was furious. Partly Falcon's doing, that—any friend of his is suspect."

Philip maintained a level gaze, aware that Roger was probing his knowledge of Falcon's affairs with Sabine. "Oh? You don't get on, then? He can be rather irritating but he is a good fellow at heart."

Roger grimaced. "I doubt that, Huntley. I do not want to quarrel with you, but I doubt it. He is an idle, scapegrace, unprincipled fellow. I only have him under my roof now for my wife's sake.

He is our nearest kin. He must be seen to acknowledge her position. After today, though—he never comes here again."

Falcon, meanwhile, had contrived to corner Sabine alone as she walked across the park to visit Jabez Starling.

She had been under the impression that Falcon had gone out with Roger and Philip and was taken aback to see him step out into her path from the copse which bordered the bailiff's house.

She stopped short, a wave of bright red running up her face.

"How much a year has altered you," he murmured, studying her face with a crooked grin. "You will note I do not say improved. I think I liked you better in your plain gowns and simplicity."

"I am sure you did," she retorted, in sudden bitterness. "I was easier prey."

He laughed admiringly. "You have more spirit than you did. If you had a fault it was in being too submissive."

Humiliation brought angry tears to her eyes. "How can you speak so to me?"

He had not intended what she read into the remark, and bit his lip, angry with himself. "I did not mean . . ." he began.

"You never mean anything," she flashed. "You are like the foam on the sea—a great deal of surface activity, but underneath—nothing."

He started towards her, involuntarily, his face taut with rage, and she shrank back from him.

For a second they looked bitterly at each other, then he let his shoulders relax and smiled.

"You have certainly changed, my dear. The little country girl would never have said that."

"I have traveled a good deal since those days," she said, with more than one meaning in her voice.

He nodded, his eyes on her face. Then he suddenly asked, "Is it my child?"

She froze, eyes wide and startled. "Your child?" she repeated numbly.

He smiled, like a cat at a mouse hole. "Yes, my dear. Is it mine?"

She laughed softly. "It is Roger's child," she said lightly. "You may be sure of that."

His brows drew together, and he stared at her. "You are sure? Quite sure, then?"

"Quite sure," she said, holding her head high.

He was silent for a second or two, then moved so quickly that she had no warning of his intention. He pinned her elbows to her sides and looked down into her face, the bright blue eyes angry, the mouth derisive.

"So you were Roger's before you were mine? Is that what I am to believe?"

"You may believe what you choose," she said breathlessly.

He pulled her closer and lowered his mouth to hers. Hard, brutal, contemptuous, his lips bruised and wounded her, his hands moving and gripping up and down her back. She did not attempt to struggle. Merely submitted without response.

When he stood back, she looked up at him scornfully.

Falcon smiled. "You fooled me once, madam. You never shall again. I have your measure now." Then he was gone.

She stood there for moments on end, fighting down tears. His contempt had burned, although she despised him herself. She was bitterly angry that he, of all people, should dare to condemn her. It was intolerable. Unjust. She decided to put off visiting Jabez and returned to the house. In her own bedroom, she walked from wall to wall struggling with emotions that exhausted and depressed her.

She had feared meeting Falcon again, conscious of the power he could maintain over her. She had been right to fear him. He had reawakened feelings and longings she had hoped dead forever. Despite her contempt and her hatred, he had only to touch her to set her pulse racing. She had been asleep, her bodily reactions dormant. Now she was wide awake, and she was terrified of the revived emotions which were now sending a trembling hunger through her body.

In this condition, she could not face going back downstairs where the hostile, curious eyes of Bella and the Amhursts would focus on her and might drag from her the secret she must at all costs hide from everyone. She particularly feared meeting Roger until she had returned to calmness.

If he so much as suspected, he might do something disastrous. His hostility towards Falcon was lulled into a dull dislike. She dared not fan it into flames once more.

When she felt a little better, she went to the nursery and comforted herself by singing lullabies to Guy, but even there his blue eyes held a constant reminder of Falcon.

The morning before they were all to leave Ceorlbury, Fanny was on her way downstairs to breakfast when she overheard a violent quarrel between Bella and Philip. Philip, of course, was attempting to calm his wife, his murmuring tones low and urgent, but she was screaming back at him.

"I am not going to be patronized in my own home by that common slut! It galls me to see her seated in my mother's chair, dispensing hospitality with all the airs of a duchess! And you do not support me as you should. You were walking in the shrubberies with Fanny half the afternoon. What are you up to, Philip? I hope you are not flirting with her. Remember, you are nothing without my money. You haven't a penny of your own."

Philip's voice answered too softly for Fanny to hear, but Bella broke in before he had finished.

"How dare you criticize me! I suppose you wish now that you had married Fanny. Her fortune is not so large, but she is ten years younger than me. That's it, isn't it? I'm too old for you. . . ." And Bella burst into frantic hiccuping tears.

Fanny did not wait to hear more. She ran, pale and shivering, down the stairs and out into the garden. Bella's outburst had been like the brutal touch of a hand upon the fragile threads of a cobweb, shattering her dream. She felt sick and humiliated. Her feelings towards Philip were too deeply embedded in her mind for her to bear to think of hostile eyes prying upon them.

Falcon was dressing when he caught a glimpse of his sister running across the lawn, her face distorted by some emotion. He frowned, hurriedly finished dressing and went out after her. She was walking round the walled rose garden, her arms huddled across her chest.

"What is it?" he asked abruptly, catching hold of her by the shoulders in order to see her face clearly.

She shook her head with a fierce refusal to speak and tried to move away.

"Something is wrong," he said in a flat tone. "Tell me, Fanny."

"Leave me alone," she almost screamed, then bit her lip in distaste of her own abandon. She would not imitate Bella by screeching like a peacock. She would be calm and in control. Only in dignity could she regain her self-respect. She drew a painful breath. "Please, Falcon. I would rather not discuss it."

He saw that she would not be moved, and slipped an arm about her comfortingly. "If you ever do want to talk about anything, Fanny, I shall listen. Remember that."

She smiled, but without real warmth because her whole being was concentrated on fighting the pain she was experiencing. "Thank you, Falcon," she said, longing for him to leave her.

He nodded, gave her another sharp glance, and left.

As soon as he was out of sight, Fanny let loose a thin, half-smothered wail of misery.

Meeting Philip in the hall, Falcon said, frowning uneasily, "Have you any idea what is wrong with Fanny? She ran out of the house just now in a state of hysteria and will not speak to me. Has something happened? Roger has not been bullying her, I suppose?"

Philip's face went even paler. Falcon had not noticed, in his anxiety over his sister, that Philip looked decidedly ill. "Perhaps Bella has quarrelled with her," Philip suggested hurriedly. "Where is Fanny now?"

"In the rose garden. Yes, Bella does seem to dislike Fanny. You may be right. Fanny detests scenes, and if Bella picked one of her arguments with her, it would make Fanny ill."

Philip stood hesitatingly on one foot, his glance sliding to the side door. "I . . . I think I'll go and talk to Fanny. I may discover what has happened."

"And I'll have a word with Bella," said Falcon grimly.

"No," said Philip in alarm. "No, Falcon, she is not well this morning. I should leave it to me. I know how to handle her."

Falcon shrugged. "Very well. But tell her I will not have her frightening my sister. Fanny is a nervous little creature at the best of times."

Philip nodded and went out into the garden.

He found Fanny seated on a wooden bench

among late-flowering red roses, her head bent over her hands in an attitude of misery that made him cross quickly to her.

He sat down beside her, his arms instinctively going out, and she, looking up in startled surprise, flushed a vivid scarlet.

"Do not look like that," he said in a rush, pulling her towards his chest.

She struggled feebly then, abandoning pretense, allowed herself to lie against him, her head beneath his chin.

"You heard us this morning?" he asked against the soft dark curls. "I thought I heard someone pass the room. You must not take Bella seriously. She strikes out at anyone when she is in one of her moods."

"She accused us . . . she said . . ." Fanny whispered chokingly, unable to speak aloud the things Bella had screamed.

"I know, I know, but it is all lies. You must not think about it again. Put it out of your head." He touched her hair in a gentle caress.

She turned her face upwards, lips pleadingly parted. "Philip," she murmured.

He drew a harsh breath, hesitated, then kissed her with such a longing, grieving gentleness that the tears rose in her eyes again even as she put one hand to his cheek.

They were so absorbed that they were unaware of a quiet figure standing in the arched gateway, watching them with disturbed eyes. Sabine had come down to pick flowers for the rose bowls in the hall. She was shocked and amazed by what she saw, and she quietly stole away again, unnoticed.

Philip lifted his head and drew back, his eyes stricken. "Fanny, I am so sorry. I should not have done that. I have no right. . . ."

She clung to him, sobbing joyfully. "My dearest," she whispered, "my dearest . . ."

"Fanny. I am Bella's husband." He stood up, white as his shirt. "I am sorry. I did not mean to do it—I lost my head. It will never happen again."

Then he was gone, striding away with a bent head, and she watched him go with eyes that ran with tears.

CHAPTER SIX

THE visitors left Ceorlbury next day at dawn, and the estate reverted to its usual calm routine. Roger plunged with relief into his outside activities. He was so weary of the continual alarms of travel that he would have been content to do nothing at all for weeks but walk around the home park inspecting timber and fencing, discussing the planting of saplings or the depredations of deer and squirrels with his keepers, feeling the steady pulse of nature restoring his peace of mind. But Sabine persuaded him to make some changes in his old style of living since the Dowager, as she had promised, had called upon them with an invitation to dinner.

"Very well," Roger sighed and was surprised to find himself enjoying the evening.

Imperceptibly he had acquired a proprietary pride in his wife. It pleased him to see her beautifully gowned at the fashionable table of the Carlews, holding her own against the other guests. It amused him to see the young men gazing adoringly at her, following raptly the turn of her honey-colored head, the dimpled smile, the soft eyes. He grew expansive over the wine when the ladies had withdrawn and invited several young fellows to shoot at Ceorlbury only to wonder, within minutes, what madness had possessed him, but yet flattered by their eager acceptance of his invitation.

Gradually a new pattern was established at the house. Roger still spent a good deal of his day out on the estate, but he no longer drank himself into a stupor before stumbling to bed. He dined out regularly with his wife, and they in their turn entertained such of the local gentry who were friendly towards them. Ceorlbury opened outwards and became involved in the life of the county as it had not been before Roger's marriage.

"You have done wonders with Roger," the Dowager told Sabine one afternoon towards Christmas. "He is a different man. He was quite the recluse before he married you. How is your son?"

"He has two teeth now," Sabine told her, smiling.

The Dowager shook her head. "I hope you do not spoil him. I never spoiled my sons—you may spoil dogs and horses, but never children. Falcon was spoiled by that doting mama of his, and look at him—bone-selfish."

Sabine bent her head over the cushion she was embroidering for Guy. Her fingers shook as she pushed the needle through the cloth. Would she never learn to control that leap of the pulse at the sound of his name!

The Dowager went on talking, apparently unaware of Sabine's silence. "I was angry with Roger when I heard he had married you, of course. I thought, as everyone else did, that you must be some scheming little hussy with ideas above her station. But I believe in smoothing over these situations. No good comes of making a public scene of one's emotions. So I insisted on coming to the christening—and I am very glad I did."

"So am I, ma'am," Sabine said gently, lifting her head to smile at her. She had grown very fond of the old Dowager during the last few months.

The old woman's face softened. She laid a hand on Sabine's knee. "You are a pretty child," she said clumsily. She found it hard to be openly affectionate and was glad to pass on to another topic. "Well, my dear, what is this gossip I hear of Fanny!"

Sabine's eyes widened as she remembered the little scene she had witnessed in the rose garden. "Fanny! Gossip!"

"They say there is an engagement afoot," the Dowager went on. "Have you heard of it?"

Sabine gave a sigh of relief. "No, ma'am. With whom?"

"Sir George Shirley. Old Northumberland family. It would be an excellent match for her. The fact is, you know, my dear, her mother was a city heiress. No family there. And although her father was an Amhurst, people are shy of marrying into trade. She will not get another chance like this one. I imagine she will jump at it."

News of Fanny's betrothal reached them two weeks later. Her mother's letter purred with good humor and self-satisfaction. She invited Roger and Sabine to a betrothal ball to be held at the London house a month later.

Roger was pleased by the engagement, but reluctant to travel to London during the worst of winter weather, and grew morose at the idea of leaving Ceorlbury again so soon.

"We need not go, surely!" Sabine said, seeing his face cloud over.

He looked shocked. "Not go! We must, of course. You will make arrangements, my dear."

Sabine, visiting the Dowager to communicate the news, asked why it was necessary for Roger to be present. "He hates the very idea of it, yet he was quite amazed when I suggested that we refuse the invitation."

"But, my dear, he is the head of the family. The Shirleys will expect it. Mrs. Amhurst has money, but no family. She must rely upon Roger to lend substance to her claim to respectability. Depend upon it, if Roger did not attend, the Shirley family would be in a mind to cry off."

"It seems ridiculous to me," said Sabine blankly.

"Society is based upon property," said the Dowager with amusement. "And the only land in the Amhurst family belongs to Roger. It reflects creditably upon him when his cousin Fanny marries into another landed family. He must be present to show a united front to the world. It is not merely Fanny marrying Sir George, you see. The Amhursts are marrying the Shirleys."

Sabine giggled. "We make less fuss when we put our ewes to the ram." Then she flushed and was relieved to see the Dowager's eyes twinkle.

"Do not say *that* to anyone but me, my love," she said, pinching Sabine's cheek.

A few days later, Roger casually mentioned that he had heard that the Fratton estate had been sold. "I wish Fratton had approached me. I would have liked to add his land to ours. It runs very conveniently to hand, and I dislike the idea of having a stranger living up on the hill above us. Fratton has not lived there in years, and I've grown accustomed to having no near neighbors, but it must change now, I suppose."

She looked up from her account book with a little frown of concentration. "Who has bought it?" She was not seriously interested, but she knew that Roger enjoyed his morning chat with her before setting out around the estate.

"It is odd, but I do not know. I met Fratton's man of business in Dorchester yesterday. He came up to me and told me the place was sold, but refused point-blank to name the buyer. Damned fellow kept grinning at me like an ape. I could make nothing of him. I only hope it is not some gimcrack merchant hoping to set up as a gentleman on his ill-gotten gains."

Sabine looked anxiously at him. A flash of suspicion had entered her head. "It is strange that he would not tell you the name."

"Oh, who is to understand the workings of a mind like that? He was always a scheming, underhanded fellow. I would not have him on my land, but Fratton was always a silly numskull."

In the following days, they heard no further news of the new owner, but Sabine could not rid herself of the uneasiness that had troubled her ever since Roger first mentioned the subject. She had no evidence on which to base her fears, but an instinct persistently suggested to her that it was Falcon who had bought Fratton's Hill. She had noticed during the christening party how Falcon had spent some time with Fratton, and, although she told herself it was sheer foolishness to suspect him, she could not forget the thought.

They were fortunate in the January weather that year. It was cold but dry, and the roads were rock hard. Guy was to be left behind at Ceorlbury, since the journey was considered too uncomfortable for him, and Sabine was unhappy at leaving him.

"Aye, aye," Roger soothed. "I know how it is with mothers. But he has a sensible nurse, and he is safer here at home than jolting over the roads with us."

She pretended compliance, but her eyes were wet as she stared back at the house when they drove away. Roger took her hand and squeezed it awkwardly. "He will do very well, my dear," he muttered.

"Yes, of course," she said, pretending still. Their relationship was as precarious as ever. She could never forget that she had been a servant in his house, that her father had been a shepherd. The education she had since received had only affected the surface of her mind. She reacted automatically with the passivity of the lower classes, accepting orders without challenge.

She was still half-afraid of him, conscious of a

darkness in him which puzzled and alarmed her. Their marriage remained one of convenience. He had never attempted to make love to her. Yet their relationship had changed. She sensed, by the way he watched her now and then, that his attitude was different. She did not quite know what to expect of him. Her own feelings were confused. She had grown accustomed to being with him all the time. She liked and admired him. Yet she was always uneasy. He was not a man who was responsive to the normal situations of life as she knew it. She did not understand his mind at all. And from incomprehension was but a short step to fear.

The journey to London was long, dull and uneventful. She remembered little of it afterwards. There were hours of jolting discomfort when she felt her head pound like the horses' hooves on the road. Hours of dragging silence when she longed for Roger to speak, yet knew, from the dark frown on his face, that he would not. Villages and towns reeled past her aching eyes. They all seemed to look alike after the first one or two. Houses, shops, people converged into a blank. At last she slept and dreamed chaotically of yet more roads, houses, villages, with a sense of looming threat constant in the background. Falcon, she thought as she woke, and then started, wondering if she had said the name aloud, but at her guilty glance, she found Roger fast asleep in his own corner, his dark head back against the squabs.

She pressed her hands to her hot cheeks. She must not allow herself to think of Falcon. She had been dreading this visit because she must be in his company, but she had determined never to be alone for an instant so as to be certain of avoiding any private meeting. She might shut him out from her sight, but his intrusive image would steal into her mind from time to time, troubling and frightening her. Her husband's dislike of him made it all the more imperative that she manage to forget him. She was afraid of what Roger might do if he suspected that Falcon and she were still involved with each other.

They had accepted Mrs. Amhurst's offer of rooms in her house. Sabine was relieved to find when they arrived that the narrow London house was by no means as awe inspiring as she had feared. After certain Venetian palaces in which they had stayed on their travels, it was almost disappointing. Tall, elegantly proportioned, the brick was already growing shabbily dirty, and the woodwork needed repainting badly.

But a footman in livery showed them obsequiously into the drawing room, and the furnishings were evidently very modern, indeed, even to Sabine's country eyes.

They stood there, shivering from a shower which had caught them as they walked up the steps, and Roger growled. "Look at that damned thing . . . chaise longue! What's wrong with a sofa? Those French things only lead to lounging and worse!"

Sabine suppressed her own admiration for the pale blue silk upholstery of the chaise longue and looked demurely about her, as though she agreed with him. The room held a number of elegant chairs and a long table on which lay books and ornaments in careful disarray. The curtains and carpet were of a soft pastel shade. A glass-fronted cabinet held small porcelain figures of shepherdesses and spaniel dogs. It was a high-ceilinged room with a flat window and stuccoed cupids and roses on the cornices, and it gave an impression of light and space which the front of the house had not implied.

Mrs. Amhurst rushed in a moment or two later and hurriedly apologized for the delay in receiving them, but, "We are so beset by callers, and the stupid servant made a mistake . . ." She had them conducted to their room to change and rest and was almost polite to Sabine in her delight at her daughter's brilliant match.

She accepted Roger's congratulations with a simper. "So kind. We are very happy, indeed. Such a grand marriage for my little Fanny . . ." her eyes flashed sidelong at Sabine, momentarily, a sneer visible in their depths. "I am sure it will be the marriage of the year. All London will be there."

While Sabine changed her gown, Roger prowled about their room, poking at various objects with distaste. "Silly, vulgar, empty-headed snob!" He stopped before Sabine. "You are not to let her upset you, d'ye hear! She is not worth it."

Their eyes met and held, hers opal, soft, puzzled; his dark and angry, yet filled with a reluctant tenderness which made her quiver.

She saw that his irritation had been all for her. He had known that she would be embarrassed, unhappy and ill at ease in this house. He resented Mrs. Amhurst's behavior towards her.

She put a hand on his arm with a slow, tentative movement. "Thank you, Roger," she whispered, smiling shyly.

His hand closed over hers. He hesitated, biting his lip, then turned away, releasing her.

She came down with him, wearing a gown of pink and white stripes, her hair dressed in the fashionable curls. A delicate necklace of gold and pearl was clasped about her neck. The fullness of her skirts emphasized her slender waist and made a soft swishing sound as she descended the stairs.

The drawing room was crowded with people who fell silent as they entered, but Roger stood close beside her, his huge shoulders seeming to protect her from their hostile gaze, and then Philip Huntley was standing in front of them, smiling.

Roger greeted him with gruff good humor. "Glad to see you, Philip. This is a grim occasion. I hate London."

Philip laughed. "You must let me take you around. I'll find something to amuse you."

"Gaming!" inquired Roger, shaking his head. "Not my line of country, my dear fellow."

"Prizefighting!" countered Philip, with an amused lift of the eyebrows.

"Ah, now that is different," Roger agreed with interest.

Philip looked at Sabine with kindness, "How is Guy?"

"Very well," she said, smiling. "And your wife, Philip?"

His cheek quivered as though a nerve jumped there, but he kept smiling. "She is here now. I am sure she will join us in a moment." He looked over his shoulder, a small frown creasing his forehead, and caught Bella's eye as she talked to some very elegant, cold-faced women on the other side of the room. Philip's jerked head signalled to her, but she turned away, lifting her chin in a sullen gesture.

He turned back, flushing. "That is Sir George Shirley's sister, the taller of the two."

"Vinegar and water," said Roger loudly, glaring across the room.

Philip grinned, relaxing a little. "I believe you, sir. Neither of the sisters is married. They live by tittle-tattle and condescension to the poor. They visit, you know, and leave soup and flannel petticoats for old ladies."

"I know the type," said Roger, bristling.

Mrs. Amhurst brought Sir George Shirley up to them a moment later, her face glowing with self-importance. Sabine disliked Sir George on sight. He was a large, heavy man, with a set of graying side whiskers and an air of patronizing conceit. His thick-fingered hands were covered with black hair on the backs, his nose bulbous and large-nostrilled.

He spoke to Roger politely but shook hands with Sabine as though he only suffered her for her husband's sake, sniffing slightly and not quite meeting her gaze.

Roger behaved impeccably under the public gaze, but Sabine saw his chin jut belligerently at Sir George's manner, and she guessed him to have taken as much a dislike to the man as she had.

His sisters came towards them, elbow to elbow, their fixed, steely smiles freezing her. She sensed their intense dislike of meeting socially someone like herself, a country girl who had been a servant, now married to a gentleman and standing in this elegant drawing room in her silk gown and gold necklace with all the air of one who had the right to be there.

The taller of the two bent her head an inch or so, no more, twitched her lips in a horrible mimicry of a smile and murmured some incoherent courtesy, one finger just touching Sabine's hand. The other followed suit, but stared at Sabine as they touched hands, her pallid blue eyes fixed and glaring.

Then in the crush of people she caught a glimpse of Falcon lounging back in a chair as he always did, his long legs stretched before him, one polished shoe over the other. He was watching her. As her eyes focused on him, she caught him off-guard, seeing the darkness of his blue eyes clearly, all the unhappiness visible there which he had not let her see on their last meeting.

She was not prepared for the rush of emotion which swamped every conscious thought like a tidal wave and, for a second or two, left her nakedly quivering, eyes wide and fixed on his, all pretense forgotten.

Everything in the room seemed to halt like a cataract frozen in midair. The very clock on the mantelpiece was silenced. Voices, faces, presences dropped away into a light from which she stared at Falcon, and knew she would only love him for the whole of her life. It was not a heated emotion. Cold, clear and unalterable, she felt it penetrating every crevice of her mind. The contempt she had felt for his seduction and later abandonment seemed meaningless now. Her own desire for him that night had been a blind physical response. Her whole past seemed a shadow compared with the crystal certainty of this moment.

Then Roger touched her elbow and spoke casually, and her flesh jerked free of the mesh of her thoughts. She blinked, feeling as though she had been roughly awakened from deep sleep. The clock resumed its ticking. The people moved and spoke again. Breathing deeply, she turned and automatically made some murmured reply to her husband which apparently satisfied him, although she had not heard his question.

She found herself facing Fanny, who was smiling shyly at her from dark-ringed, unhappy eyes.

They sat down together on one of the chaise longues, Fanny arranging her green-striped gown with the precision and care of someone trying to force down misery.

Sabine watched her closely, wondering how Falcon could allow his sister to enter into a betrothal that so clearly made her unhappy. Glancing across the room, she caught Philip Huntley's anxious eyes upon them. He looked away immediately, a small flush rising on his cheeks, and she frowned.

"How is Guy?" Fanny asked politely.

"Very well," Sabine answered, still watching her, "I hope you will be happy, Fanny. Have you known Sir George long?"

Fanny plaited her fingers carefully. "For several years or so."

"Do you mean to live in London after the marriage?"

"No, Sir George prefers to live in Northumberland. I imagine we shall visit London every year, but we shall make our home on his estate, of course." Fanny seemed indifferent, as though she spoke to someone else, and her voice was dull and flat.

"When do you plan to have the wedding?"

"Sir George wishes to have the private apartments at the castle refurbished before we are married, so we intend to wait for some months. And, of course, there is always so much to do before a wedding."

"Do you mean to go abroad for your bridal tour?"

"No," Fanny said, in that same dead voice. "Sir George does not like traveling on the Continent. We shall leave at once for Northumberland."

For a moment or two, Sabine stared at her. Fanny had the look of passive despair she had once seen on the face of a caged monkey in Genoa, staring out through the bars with dark, suffering eyes at a hostile world, yet accepting its impotence to change its condition.

Do I look like that, she wondered? Then she regretted the thought. Roger was a good man, and she owed him too much to allow herself to resent the fact that she was his wife. He had saved her life, protected her with his name, showered her with loving kindness. It was selfish and wicked of her to lack gratitude.

Falteringly, she asked Fanny, "You . . . you are happy?"

The other girl looked startled and a very faint color came back into her cheeks. "I . . ." she stammered, then very quickly said, "Of course! How could I not be? It is a great honor for me to marry Sir George. He could pick anyone in London, but he picked me." She was repeating her mother's words to her without realizing it, and her voice took on her mother's intonation unconsciously, while her eyes slid round the room with a guilty look to where Mrs. Amhurst was proudly showing off Sir George to a new arrival.

Sabine sighed. She was not sufficiently in Fanny's confidence to press the matter and must accept what she was told. But she could not help wishing there was something she could do for this unhappy girl. She felt angrily helpless in the face of a social convention that forbade her to pry into Fanny's hidden emotions. The whole basis of the society into which her marriage had brought her seemed to her to be a furtive hypocrisy. It must be plain to everyone that Fanny loathed Sir George, yet they all pretended to believe her a lucky girl to be marrying him.

Had Fanny been living in poverty, her conduct might be excusable, but Sabine knew that the Amhursts had a great fortune. Why was Fanny doing this?

Suddenly Sabine was very still, her face drawn and tense. Could it be possible that Fanny was marrying for the same reason that she had married Roger? She remembered that little scene in the rose garden. Philip Huntley's arms around Fanny, hers clinging round his neck. Could that be the explanation? Was Fanny carrying a child?

Philip Huntley kept his word the next morning and carried Roger off to see a prizefight in the East End of London. Fanny and Sabine went shopping together for hats in the fashionable modistes of the West End of the town and, laden with hatboxes, returned in a rather more cheerful mood than they had set out. Buying hats was, Sabine saw, an occupation calculated to raise the most gloomy spirits.

"Is my mama upstairs, Fanton?" Fanny asked the butler with a little smile.

"No, Miss Fanny. She is visiting Lady Alvrey today, if you recall," he answered.

The ball was to be held two days later, but the household was already in the throes of making the arrangements. Straw was to be laid in the street outside. Extra footmen had been engaged for the evening. The caterers were spoken for, and the champagne ordered. The servants darted constantly about the house like bees buzzing excitedly, and meals were apt to be haphazard affairs as the kitchen was busy with the preparation of such of the food as was to be made on the premises.

All this was in the butler's manner as he waited for Fanny and Sabine to go upstairs, shifting from one foot to the other impatiently.

Fanny went to her room to change, taking her new hats with her so that she might try them on again in the privacy of her bedroom.

Sabine went into her own room and stopped on the threshold as she saw Falcon sitting on the small, gold-painted chair by her bed.

He rose, bowing ironically.

She closed the door with a nervous backward glance and leaned against it, looking at him.

"You must be mad to come here! It would ruin me if anyone saw you in my room."

"Only your own maid is likely to come in here," he retorted. "And she, I believe, is devoted to you, or so the servants inform me."

She automatically began to remove her hat, standing at a distance from him. "What do you want?"

"To see you," he drawled, still mocking, but with that darkened look of the eyes which made her pulse beat faster.

"You must go," she said sharply.

"Did you enjoy your shopping expedition with Fanny?" he asked, smiling, as though this were a normal polite chat in the drawing room.

"Why are you allowing her to marry that man?" Sabine asked in sudden irritation. "You must know she detests him. She is almost mad with misery. The merest stranger could see it."

Falcon sat up, surprised. "Fanny? Unhappy?"

Sabine saw that he had not had any idea of it. "She is your sister—you should look at her once in a while," she said angrily.

He frowned. "What has she said to you?"

"Nothing," Sabine said scornfully. "There was no need. I only had to look at her."

"She was not forced to accept Shirley, if that is what you think," he said. "I gave my permission when it was requested. I had no more to do with it than that. My mother is hot for it, but Fanny is not a child. She could have refused him."

"When she is in love with someone else?" Sabine suggested.

He looked baffled. "I do not follow you."

"Fanny is in love with another man," she said, hoping that Fanny would forgive her for this interference. She could see from Falcon's face that he knew nothing of all this, and she hoped that once he knew, he might do something to help his sister.

"How do you know? And if she is, why should she marry Shirley? I do not understand what you are trying to say."

"He is married," she said slowly, and, at his look of angry disbelief, "Oh, Fanny would deny it if you asked, and, to be frank, I do not think that it should have a bearing on the situation except in so far as it explains her acceptance of a marriage that makes her deeply unhappy. I only tell you so that you may understand why she accepted Sir George."

"She has told you all this? You know whom she loves? She had been having an affair with a married man—is that what you are telling me? Good God, do you expect me to believe that of my sister?" He was starkly angry now, his mouth taut and white.

She shook her head and said quickly, "No, I do not say that there has been any improper behavior. One may be in love without that." And for a second, her eyes flashed contempt at him, and, catching it, his face glowed with bitter regret.

He stood up and walked to the window. For a moment, they were both silent. Then he turned. "Do I know this man?"

She did not answer, but their eyes met in a long look, and his face suddenly altered. She saw the thought move into his mind.

"I know him," he said slowly. "Good God! I have been blind. Under my very eyes all this time. Once or twice some faint suspicion crossed my mind, but I was too selfishly absorbed with my own life to connect them up. Fanny and Philip!" He looked hard at her. "It is, isn't it? Fanny and Philip? What a fool I have been! How stupidly obsessed with myself not to notice. The way they look at each other. Silences. Only the other day, I mentioned him, and she changed color. I noticed it without even thinking."

"You must help her," Sabine urged. "If she

marries Sir George, she will be so unhappy! You must stop the marriage."

"How can I?" Falcon said, half to himself. "It is all arranged. Settled. There would be the most terrible scandal. And would Fanny agree to it? She must have thought seriously before accepting him. She cannot hope to marry Philip. Who am I to say she is not right to remove herself from his company like this?"

"If Sir George were any other man, she might be right—but she detests him!" Sabine urged angrily.

Falcon sighed. "I must admit I do not care for him myself. But all the same. . . ."

"Consider her life in the future," Sabine pressed. "Married to a man she can neither respect nor like! The idea is intolerable."

"Why do you feel so strongly?" he asked abruptly, his old, intimate look returning. "What does it mean to you if Fanny makes a mess of her life? You barely know her."

She turned away from that ironic, close regard. "I am sorry for her. She is caught in a trap of circumstance, as I once was, and has taken the first way out which presented itself."

He was at her side now, his hand seeking hers, his head bent over her. "As you did? Sabine, as you did? Don't push me away. Listen to me. . . ." His voice was husky and uncertain. "Forgive me. I cannot bear this distance between us. I know that what I did was unforgivable, but I did not mean to do it. I intended no wrong to you. I lost my head. I was drunk . . ."

Illogically, his protests angered her. It seemed
to add insult to injury for him to say he had not
intended to seduce her. She snatched her hand
away from him and walked to the door.

"You had better leave now before my husband
returns." She emphasized the word husband with
a look of bitter coldness and saw with painful
triumph the wince that it produced.

He obeyed in silence, and when he had gone
she leaned against the door, breathing as though
she had been running.

CHAPTER SEVEN

SHE did not understand herself. The swings of her moods were inexplicable and contrary, affected by the merest feather in the balance. She loved, yet resented her love, and she was shocked by the fierce pleasure it had given her to see Falcon wince at her mention of Roger. This desire to wound, which she had only lately discovered in herself, puzzled and disturbed her. She was not cruel by nature, she told herself angrily. She had been warped by events.

She flung herself down on her bed and stared at the curtains moving in a slight breeze, the distant sounds of London's streets coming faintly now and then. She smiled, remembering her childhood when the high bleating of lambs had been the only sound she could hear as she lay awake in the early mornings. How long ago that seemed now. How much had happened to her. Was she even the same person? Sometimes it seemed to her that she had died, as herself, on the evening when she tried to drown herself, and that from that day a totally new personality had inhabited her body. She ran an exploratory finger over her face, feeling the new, sharper lines of cheek and jaw, the wary set of the mouth drawn in at the corners with distrust and restraint. As a young girl, her

face had been soft and innocent, plastic with
ignorance. Now it had an adult hardness. The
curves of girlhood had gone, leaving the bones
more prominent, the eyes defiant and carefully
shielded from probing curiosity, the whole impression of the face now being of a tough aware-
ness and control.

When Roger returned from his prizefight he
found her dressing for dinner. Marette was soberly
buttoning the dark green checked evening gown,
her heavy face set in gentler lines, as it always
was when she was with her mistress.

"A capital day," Roger pronounced, grinning
at Sabine. He was flushed and in obvious good
spirits.

She smiled at him in her mirror, touched by his
almost childlike pleasure.

He fished into his pocket and produced a flat
box, from which, smiling, he drew a pretty silver
necklace, set with opals which sparkled as he
swung it on his finger, changing color all the time,
from blue to green and then a rosy pink.

Marette turned to look closer, and her dark
face grew heavier. "Opals! They are dangerous
stones," she muttered to herself. "Evil fortune
comes with them. . . ."

Slightly drunk, Roger laughed, "What a piece
of nonsense, woman! Opals are lucky." He held
the necklace, still swinging, near Sabine's face,
bending to see her in the mirror. "See, they match
her lovely eyes," he said with satisfaction, and
ducked his head to kiss her bare white shoulder in
a sudden movement which made her stiffen.

He straightened, even more flushed, and laughed again, not quite meeting her eyes. Fumblingly, he clasped the necklace around her throat and stood back to survey the result. Sabine shivered as the cold metal settled against her skin, but she smiled stiffly at him and thanked him.

Marette watched with alert attention. She had no illusions about the relations between her master and mistress. Her practical French mind saw nothing strange in a marriage of convenience, but it puzzled her that these two had produced a child, yet now did not live together as man and wife. What had happened to produce this rift between them, she wondered, slowly looking from Roger's elated, flushed face to Sabine's pale, set features? And why was there a look of sadness always at the back of her mistress's eyes?

Roger began to talk about the prizefight he had seen, talking in the queer, technical slang used by the *cognoscenti* when they discussed this brutal sport. Sabine pretended interest but longed for him to remove himself. More and more, lately, she was forced to realize that her husband was becoming attracted to her. His kiss, just now, had been an overt attention that underlined what she had already suspected. Listening with apparent fascination to his noisy talk, she kept her eyes half-veiled to disguise their expression from him. She was afraid. Yet how, in honesty, could she refuse him if he came to her bed one night? She owed him too much to be able to do that.

Fanny, too, was dressing in her room, sitting dispiritedly under her maid's deft hands as the woman twisted her brown hair into the fashionable curls she affected. A tap on the door made her jump, and when Falcon put his head inside and asked for a private word with her, she frowned but sent her maid away.

His expression alarmed her. "What is it? You are very pale. Is something wrong?"

He sat down with his usual lounging grace in the tiny chair which stood beside the dressing table and watched her from beneath his hooded lids.

"Fan, are you determined on this marriage?" he asked in a brusque tone.

She looked taken aback, and a faint tide of pink crept up her face. "That is an odd question at this stage. What do you mean, Falcon?" She pretended to laugh. "You gave your permission weeks ago, you know."

"I was too selfishly absorbed in my own affairs to have thought seriously about the idea," he said bluntly. "But I have been thinking recently, and, to be frank, I cannot like Sir George. I find him unpleasant. And I am afraid you will not be happy with him." He was still watching her closely, his face intent. "I am sorry to be so blunt, but I think it time for honesty between us, Fan. You are my sister. I should have been more careful of you."

She was as white now as she had just been pink. "If you had spoken earlier! But it is too late now." She drew a quivering breath, her hands clenching, "I cannot break off now. It has gone too far."

He leaned forward, the lazy pose gone and his eyes serious. "It is not too late. If you dislike him, you must not marry him. It would be madness. Do not be afraid to be honest with me, Fanny."

His gentle tones moved her, breaking down the barrier she had set up between herself and the world. "Oh, Falcon," she whispered, "I do not know what to do. But I could not break off. Mama would never forgive me."

"Leave Mama to me," he said lightly, smiling. "Do not think of other people. Think of yourself."

"How can I?" she answered miserably. "You have not considered what would follow if I jilted Sir George. The scandal. The gossip." She put her hands over her face and rubbed her eyes, like a child. "I could not bear it."

"None of that matters," he dismissed. "All that concerns me is your happiness."

"I could not be happy if I were a social outcast," she wailed. "Knowing myself the topic of conversation in every club in London! The shame would kill me."

He saw that she was determined, and he stood up. "I will leave you to think about it. If you change your mind, come to me, and I will help you. I only want your happiness, you know."

Her stubborn look melted. She smiled, half-tearful. "Oh, Falcon, how kind you are—I had not expected such understanding from you. I have misjudged you."

He grimaced wryly. "No, my dear, I think not.

I have been blindly selfish, but it was not deliberate. Mere stupidity."

She laughed, shaking her head. "No, you are too good. I only wish I had known before that I might trust you."

He sat down again, suddenly, taking her hand and leaning towards her confidentially, "Trust me now. Tell me why you accepted Sir George when you dislike him so? Tell me why you look so sad?"

She pressed his fingers, shaking her head. "I have been very silly. I accepted him on an impulse and have been regretting it ever since."

"There is nothing more you wish to tell me?" he pressed, smiling warmly and invitingly at her. "Do not be afraid, Fan, I guarantee I am unshockable."

She flushed, dropping her gaze. "No," she said quickly. "No, there is nothing more to tell."

He waited a moment, then sighed. "Very well. But remember, Fan. You can trust me."

When the door had closed behind him, she let out a long, harsh breath, and a sob racked her, the tears trickling out of her eyes and sliding down her cheeks.

Falcon went downstairs and met Philip in the hall. He shot him a curiously hard look, hesitated, then said, "I have been looking for you. Will you come out for a stroll before dinner? I have something to discuss with you in private."

Philip looked surprised, but agreed at once, and they went out and strolled along the gravel paths between the ornamental shrubs at the back of the house, which served as some form of garden.

Falcon was half-reluctant to open the topic. He felt himself in part responsible for what had happened. Had he not interfered in Philip's life by bringing him down to Ceorlbury to meet Bella, the situation would not have arisen. Philip had on several occasions attempted to break free of the engagement to Bella, and he had persuaded him otherwise. He remembered with bitter regret his casual dismissal of Philip's question as to whether Fanny might be prepared to marry him. Had he known, then, that Philip was seriously interested in his sister, he might have encouraged a betrothal between them. But, ignorant of Philip's feelings, he had merely looked about for a rich prize for him and chosen the very first person Philip should have married.

Philip was looking at him sidelong, his pleasant face puzzled and a little amused. "You look very grim, Falcon. What is wrong? What was it you wanted to discuss?"

"Fanny," said Falcon abruptly, deciding to take the bull by the horns.

Philip stopped dead in his tracks and turned to look at him, going pale. "What?"

Falcon met his eyes coolly. "I do not know what there has been between you, but I am aware that there has been something," he said flatly.

Hotly, Philip retorted, "If you are suggesting that Fanny, of all people, would ever stoop to doing anything wrong . . ."

"I hope I know my sister better than that, blind though I may have been as to her state of feeling," drawled Falcon.

Philip bit his lip. "Then what?"

"You are in love, Philip?" Falcon asked, quite gently.

For a moment, Philip was silent, then he turned and walked on slowly. "Yes," he said in a quiet tone.

"And Fanny returns your love," Falcon added, catching up with him. "And, being Fanny, tried to redeem herself by accepting the abominable Sir George."

"I imagine so," Philip agreed, his face setting in weary lines. "Though why you permitted it, God knows."

"Folly, my dear Philip, folly. I was too concerned with my own misery to be aware of Fanny's."

Philip's expression softened. "Yes. I am sorry. It is still the same with you, then? You had not mentioned it lately. I was hoping you had got over that."

Falcon laughed dryly. "One might as well hope to get over being alive. The condition has the same almost enviable conclusion. I shall stop loving Sabine when I stop breathing. Never before." He turned and looked at his friend grimly. "And you, Philip?"

"The same," said Philip.

Falcon grinned harshly. "What a pair we are! God, Philip, why did you not tell me to mind my own business when I tried to pair you off with Bella? You loved Fanny then, I presume?"

"And thought it hopeless," said Philip. "She had never looked at me. She was so young and so rich. I did not dare to hope. Ironically, it was only when I was married that I began to see a great deal of her, and she began to . . ." he stopped, grimacing.

"What a mess," Falcon ground out angrily. "I blame myself for it all. I shall never interfere in other people's lives again, I assure you."

Philip smiled wearily. "How can you be so foolish, Falcon? It was mere chance that you brought Bella and me together. I might as easily have married elsewhere without your help. I was on the lookout for a wife, as you well know."

"I pushed you into Bella's arms," Falcon insisted. "You wanted to back out at one time, but I would not let you."

"Well, never mind that," said Philip, indifference in his tone. "What are you going to do about Fanny? I did not dare to speak before for fear of rousing your suspicions, but I cannot think this a suitable marriage." He reddened and looked uncomfortable, adding, "Do not think I would dislike any marriage she might make. I realize she must marry, but . . ."

"I know," Falcon agreed. "Sir George Shirley is a pompous, narrow-minded brute. I have not liked him since I overheard his comments about Sabine two days since. Fanny must not marry him."

"You will tell her so?" asked Philip eagerly.

"I have already done so, but she refuses to listen. She is afraid of the gossip."

"You must persuade her to it," said Philip with alarm.

"My sister, I have discovered, may look like an angel, but she has the temperament of a stubborn mule when she so chooses," Falcon murmured. "That is why I want you to see her and talk her round."

"I?" Philip was suddenly white. "My God, I could not even broach the subject. Have you any conception of what you ask of me?"

"She would listen to you," urged Falcon, uncomprehendingly.

Philip laughed, his face twisted with pain. "She has not spoken to me for months."

Falcon stared. "What?"

"Oh, in public she is polite," Philip added. "But she speaks to me as though I were the merest stranger, and if we are left alone for so much as a second, she runs away like a scalded cat. It would be impossible for me to talk to her on this subject, on any subject."

"Then what is to be done?"

"I hesitate to suggest it," Philip murmured. "But . . . Sabine?"

Falcon looked sharply at him. "You think Fanny would listen to her? But they barely know each other." He hesitated, his jaw grim, then plunged on, "It was Sabine who first opened my eyes to Fanny's unhappiness. She seems to be aware that Fanny loves you. I do not know how far she is in Fanny's confidence, but she clearly felt she could not deal with it herself, or she would not have spoken to me."

"She knew?" Philip repeated curiously. "That is strange. I would not have expected Fanny to confide in anyone."

Falcon laughed. "I long ago decided I would never understand women. They tell each other secrets that a man would go to the stake to defend."

"If you wish," Philip said uneasily, "I will speak to Sabine about Fanny."

Falcon shook his head. A strange little smile twisted his mouth. "No, Philip. I will deal with it. I will speak to her tomorrow at the ball."

Philip sighed.

The ball was a glittering occasion. The whole of the ground floor of the house had been thrown into one room for the evening by removal of the folding partition that separated the dining room from the drawing room, and a small band of musicians had been set up at one end of the ballroom thus created. Tubs of flowers stood about the house, filling the air with a thick sweet perfume, and hired chairs were put out along the walls. Wooden-faced footmen seemed to spring up out of the ground at every turn, and, as each guest arrived, Sabine, watching from a vantage point, wondered how many more people the narrow house could possibly accommodate.

Fanny and her mother stood with Falcon, welcoming the guests. Sir George, placed at Fanny's elbow, patronized her with a self-satisfied smirk when she looked up at him from time to time.

"I detest the fellow," Roger told Sabine, scowling. "But it is a good match for Fanny. Gives her consequence."

Bella and Philip joined them a moment later. Bella was wearing an overornate gown of deep puce trimmed with gray and looked rather hectic, a bright spot of color burning in each cheek.

She talked loudly and excitedly to Roger, holding Philip's arm in a proprietary gesture which made him look rather foolish, like a pet dog on a short leash. He smiled sheepishly at Sabine when their eyes met, and she returned the smile, feeling very sorry for him.

The ball was opened by Fanny and Sir George, and soon the room was crowded with elegant persons all determined to squeeze the utmost enjoyment from their evening. Dancing somehow continued, despite the crush, and the musicians perspired like madmen as their services were enthusiastically applauded between dances.

Roger, having stood up with Sabine for the cotillion, retired gratefully to the card room where, with other gentlemen, he sat down to a game of whist in a more peaceful atmosphere.

Seizing the opportunity of speaking to Fanny, Sabine observed how pale she looked even tonight, in the hothouse atmosphere of the overcrowded ballroom. While they were exchanging meaningless small talk, Bella crossed to speak to them, all smiles, and whispered that she had something very exciting to tell them both.

Fanny looked politely uneasy. Sabine, to cover for her, asked with pretended enthusiasm what Bella meant, and Bella beamed.

"I visited my doctor this morning," Bella whispered, leaning her head towards Sabine. "And you may imagine my delight when he confirmed my own suspicions!" She nodded vigorously as Sabine, eyes wide, opened her mouth to speak, and then closed it again.

"Aye, it is really true! I am to have a child!"

"How delightful," Sabine managed to say, smiling falsely, before Philip appeared and took Bella away with him to dance.

Then Sabine turned to look at Fanny and was deeply alarmed to find her white and limp, on the point of fainting.

She quickly supported her with an arm around her waist. To the queries of their near neighbors, she returned the reply that Fanny was feeling the heat, and began to half carry, half lead her from the ballroom.

Falcon met them halfway and, seizing Fanny, took her weight entirely, and soon extricated them from the crush.

He then lifted the girl into his arms and carried her up the stairs, Sabine following automatically.

When he had laid Fanny on her bed, he looked round at Sabine. "What has happened?"

"The heat . . ." she lied.

He dipped his handkerchief in a bowl of water from Fanny's washstand and gently wiped her face.

She opened her eyes, breathing lightly, looked

up and gave a vague smile. "I am so sorry to be a nuisance. I do not know what made me behave so foolishly."

"You must rest for a while," he said gently. "Lie there. I will make your excuses downstairs."

"No, no," she said, struggling to sit up. "It would look so rude . . ."

He made her lie down again with a firm but kind hand. "Do as I tell you, Fan. You may come down after supper."

She relaxed again, sighing, grateful to be overruled, and Falcon led Sabine quietly out of the room.

He stood on the landing looking down at her, one brow raised. "Well? What really happened? I saw her face while Bella was talking to you. What was she saying?"

Sabine told him, and he whistled softly. "That is the devil!"

She nodded. "I must go down again," she said, stepping round him, but he caught at her arm.

"Wait. I wanted a word with you about Fanny, anyway."

"Oh?" She stood, poised on one foot, looking warily at him.

"I spoke to her and found that you were quite right in your suspicions. She is desperately unhappy, but she obstinately refuses to break off the marriage. I want you to speak to her . . ."

"She would not listen to me!" said Sabine in amazement. "And I have no right to mention the subject to her. It is out of the question."

"Someone must make her see sense," he said,

"especially after tonight. I will take her away for a year, to Europe, if she wishes. Will you tell her that?"

She shook her head. "You must see that I cannot do so."

He sighed. "Then I shall have to tackle her again myself."

Sabine nodded. "That is far the best idea." She could hear the gay swirl of a waltz tune below and added, "I must go down. I am booked to dance this with Philip."

Falcon said huskily, "Dance a few bars with me, first," and deftly slid his arm around her waist.

She stiffened at the touch of his hand and put her own hand to push him away, but he caught it in his own and swayed her into the waltz.

She was surprised into acquiescence for a moment, acutely conscious of his arm around her, his shoulder near her face. He danced well, and she allowed herself to surrender briefly to the pleasure of matching her steps to his, before forcing herself to break out of the trance which threatened to overwhelm her.

"No," she breathed, pulling herself out of the circle of his arm.

He sighed and let his arm fall.

She turned and ran lightly down the stairs, leaving him leaning against the wall, breathing fast.

Then he slowly returned to Fanny's room, knocked and went inside.

She looked at him, her lids faintly wet, the pale lashes stuck together.

He pulled up a chair and sat down, his hands on his knees. "Fanny," he said softly, "you are ill."

She blinked. "What?"

"Far too ill to get up again tonight. I shall send for Dr. Parsons, and he will tell Mama and Sir George that you have some debilitating disease which necessitates a long sea voyage." He paused, smiling at Fanny. "We shall go together, you and I, Fanny. We shall be away for a year, at least, and when we are on the other side of the world, we shall write to Sir George, breaking off the betrothal with great regret, but making it clear that your health would not permit you to marry for a long time."

Fanny's cheeks were filling with color, and her eyes were becoming bright, but she said faintly, "We could not!"

"We shall," said Falcon firmly, "I have given a great deal of thought to this. Now, lie back and look very ill indeed. Have you any rice powder? Good, then give yourself a deathly pallor and, whatever Mama says, refuse to get up. You are very, very ill." He bent over her and kissed her. "Do you understand, Fan?"

"You are too kind to me," Fanny said, tearfully. "Thank you, Falcon."

He smiled. "We shall enjoy our sea voyage enormously, I promise you."

The ball proceeded downstairs with the same gaiety, the chattering guests only faintly aware of something unusual going on underneath the bright surface.

The doctor arrived, and Mrs. Amhurst, hot-cheeked and furious, argued with Falcon when he refused to let her go upstairs to Fanny.

"She cannot be ill!" she said shrilly. "Fanny was never ill in her life! She has taken one of her crotchets, and you must defend her! I was never so humiliated. The house full of people, her betrothal to be announced, and Fanny takes to her bed! Both my children conspire to be ungrateful."

"Mama," Falcon said firmly, "Fanny has collapsed. I am afraid for her lungs."

"Her lungs?" shrieked Mrs. Amhurst in horror.

"You remember, our Aunt Bathhurst once had consumption," he said, sighing. "Fanny has just that wan look!"

Mrs. Amhurst looked distractedly about her. "What shall we do? Sir George! The guests! Oh, was anything ever so provoking! I do not know how I shall stand it! I shall go to bed! My head aches. I am ill myself."

"No, Mama," he said sternly. "You will see Sir George. Explain the circumstances. Tell him Fanny has collapsed with what we fear to be lung fever. There will be no announcement tonight."

"No announcement? No announcement? Oh, God, my head!" she moaned, tottering.

Falcon caught sight of Philip tactfully hovering at a distance and beckoned to him. He apprised him of the situation in a few quick words and confided his mother to Philip's willing care, then he returned upstairs to Fanny.

CHAPTER EIGHT

THE rest of the evening was unbearable for Mrs. Amhurst, who had to carry the weight of the curious questions of her guests while striving to pacify Sir George who, conscious of his own appearance in the affair, was deeply mortified by his betrothed's strange disappearance just before the announcement was to be made. He was a man to whom dignity meant more than anything else. He resented Fanny's collapse as though it were a personal insult, and since his sister thoroughly concurred in his attitude, he was stiffly angry when he left the house that night.

"She has ruined herself!" Mrs. Amhurst moaned to Philip, leaning on his arm as though she were a very old woman.

"No, no," he soothed, "society has a short memory."

"Sir George hasn't," she said, truthfully. "And he will never forgive her! He will not marry her now. I am certain of it. She will be an old maid. Why are my children so wicked? Falcon threw away his chance of inheriting Ceorlbury on a mere whim, and now Fanny ruins her chance of being mistress of Shirley Castle. I am distracted. I shall never recover. I must go and lie down." And she allowed him to lead her, tottering, to the stairs.

155

Philip rejoined Falcon. Deeply relieved by this turn of events, he smiled at him, "How is Fanny now?"

"A great deal worse," answered Falcon solemnly. "I am afraid for her life."

Philip was white at once. "Good God, what is wrong with her? I had thought it a mere excuse."

"So it is," Falcon nodded, grinning, "but my mother must not know. I plan to carry Fanny off on a sea voyage. We may then break the betrothal without having to bear the consequent scandal."

Bella bore down upon them and seized Philip's arm. "What is going on? Is Fanny truly very ill? I am feeling quite weak, myself, and in my condition I should not overtax my strength you know, Philip."

He pretended deep concern and tenderly led her away. Falcon watched them with pity. Poor Philip, he thought. What a life he must lead!

Sabine was sitting on the far side of the emptying ballroom, slowly fanning herself, her face flushed. She had danced energetically for the last half of the evening and was now very tired, but Roger showed no signs of tiring of his card games.

She was aware of Falcon's approach although she never once looked in his direction, and her pulse leaped as he sat down beside her, stretching out his long legs with a weary sigh.

He told her of the arrangements he had made to take Fanny away at once.

"When do you and Roger return to Dorset?" he asked, after a pause.

"I think we will leave tomorrow, now. This

house will be in uproar, I imagine, when Mrs. Amhurst discovers your plans."

"Sabine," he said, huskily, "you do believe that I bitterly repent what I did? Tell me that you forgive me. We may not meet again for a year. Tell me you forgive me."

She had been thinking gently of him during the last hour, but now that he was actually with her, she found herself bitterly angry again. He had ruined her lightly and then deserted her, yet he asked her to forgive him as though it had been some small social misdemeanor he had committed. I hate him, she thought savagely. I hate him.

She did not answer, turning her head away, her eyes burning with fury.

In a tone almost humble, he pleaded, "What can I do to prove to you how I feel? Can you fail to understand that it is punishment enough for me to have lost you by my own folly? If I had the chance again, do you think I would let you go?"

"Your feelings can be of no interest to me," she said icily, rising.

He followed her, silenced, and stood in the hall watching with a grim expression as she went up the stairs, the trailing skirts swishing over the treads. Had there been no footmen watching, he would have followed her, but he could do nothing under their wooden stare but retreat again to the ballroom.

In her own room, Sabine sank onto her bed, her arms clutching her shoulders, shuddering with the aftereffects of the scene. Had Falcon come to her then, he would have seen her in a different mood.

Love and despair left her helpless, like a shorn lamb in icy winds, and she broke down in silent sobbing against her pillows. Marette found her there and watched darkly, her thick fingers gentle against her mistress's curls, soothing her into an exhausted sleep.

Mrs. Amhurst was not visible next day when Roger and Sabine left for Ceorlbury. She had taken to her bed, and would not get up. Falcon said the farewells, his hooded eyes disguising the misery only Sabine suspected. Roger was roughly, reluctantly polite, but he was glad to be on his way home again. He was baffled by Fanny's collapse and felt that he had been brought up to London on false pretenses since no announcement of the betrothal had been made. He climbed on to the seat opposite his wife, sighing with relief, and grunted a reply to Falcon's last words.

The door shut, and the horses plunged forward.

Sabine glanced sidelong, beneath her lashes, for a last glimpse of Falcon, and, without being aware of it, betrayed herself by the hunger of her expression. He stiffened, his jaw tightening, and a light came into the vivid blue eyes.

Then they were out of sight, and she sank back, breathing deeply.

Roger met her gaze, his black brows drawn thickly over his eyes. He, too, had seen that last exchange of glances, and his face was set.

She flushed and looked away, conscious of his suspicious gaze.

The return journey was far worse than they had

expected. A sudden drop in temperature brought
a flurry of snow which, as the miles fell away,
thickened into a blizzard. They only just reached
Ceorlbury in time. That night the snow fell without pause, and in the morning they awoke to a
white world.

Sabine, reunited with Guy, watched with him
from the nursery window as the great white flakes
dropped past, coating trees and houses.

Guy wriggled and shouted with joy when she
opened the window to let him feel the icy pleasure
of a snowflake melting on his tongue. He put his
plump little hand out and laughed as the cold
whiteness drifted and melted against him.

One of the keepers trudged past, some dogs at
his heels, his head hooded, his shoulders hunched,
feet sinking into the drifts. The bare, black trees,
their branches brushed with white on one side,
were alive with shivering birds sitting hunched
against the wind. The shrubberies were trans-
formed into weird galleries of snowmen as each
bush was buried beneath a crystalline coating
through which protruded bare twigs, or shrivelled
leaves, or the glossy dark green of the laurels when
the snow slid off and left them visible again.

Roger was different since their return from
London. Sabine wished she could read his mind,
but since they still lived separately under one
roof, she could only guess at what he thought.

She was correct in suspecting that he desired
to make her a normal wife, at last. He had been
gradually more and more attracted to her, and

during their stay in London he had watched her closely when she was with Falcon.

That some deep relationship existed between them had been obvious to him, but he had not been certain as to what it meant until the last moments.

At times he had been certain Sabine hated and despised Falcon. At others he had feared she was still attracted to him. But that brief glance of hers, sudden and secret, had told him more than any mere circumstantial evidence could. There had been passion, grief, longing, in her eyes.

It had been a shock to him. He had allowed himself to believe that Sabine's seduction two years earlier had been against her will. He had convinced himself of her innocence, her virtue, and had hoped to teach her to love him in time.

Now he had to face the truth. Sabine loved Falcon. Always had loved him. She might hate him for his desertion of her, but she still responded to him.

Roger's own dislike of Falcon had grown during the last two years. His contempt for the other man's town attitudes had been only the basis on which a fierce antagonism could grow. Jealousy, personal hostility, fed the weed over the months, and now Roger hated his cousin with an obsessive bitterness.

The winter, having set in, froze over and made the roads impassable and the river a gray-green sheet of ice.

The local children skated on it during the short, cold days, the park ringing with their distant laughter. Sabine remembered her own childhood as she listened to them and yearned for the simple innocence of other days.

In March news came of her father's death far away in the north, and she went into mourning for him. He left her nothing but his old Bible, much-thumbed, and that she placed upon her bedroom table where it reminded her daily of things she had begun to forget. Of the eweleaze in spring, when lambs skipped over the greening grass bleating; of Sundays when she walked to church in a clean gown; of harvest suppers and singing and pails of creamy warm milk. It was all she had left of her childhood now, and, having lost it all, she saw that the gloominess of her father's temper had never quite dampened the beauty she found around her. As she got older, she remembered more of the good things, less of the bad.

They heard from the Dowager in April that Mrs. Amhurst had taken Fanny to the West Indies to visit a distant cousin who lived there.

"They say Fanny is in poor health and must travel abroad to regain her spirits," the Dowager told them.

Sabine asked her when they were alone if Falcon had gone with his mother and sister, but the Dowager believed not. "I gather the marriage to Sir George Shirley will not now take place," she said disapprovingly. "It is a pity."

Sabine did not repeat to Roger what the Dowager had said of Falcon, and he continued to believe that Falcon, too, was in the West Indies.

His temper improved in consequence, and he

took Sabine and Guy to Weymouth for a week in early May.

She was very much attached to this elegant little watering place, once so popular with George III, and enjoyed her stay there enormously. Guy was both fascinated and terrified by the great, blue, rolling waves which seemed so huge to him, falling from the great height as they advanced over the sands.

The days were warm and sunny and since it was early in the season there were few visitors in the narrow little streets, so they were able to enjoy their stay without any of the discomforts suffered by those who came in high season.

They drove out to Portland to see the naval dockyard and Guy was enchanted by some merry sailors who teased and flattered him, carrying him about on their shoulders to show him various sights. Sabine, naturally, was much admired, and Roger scowled when one particularly charming officer suggested she allow him to row her out to view his ship. She refused sweetly, to Roger's great relief.

They returned to Ceorlbury regretfully, more united as a family than they had ever been before, but the harmony was not to last. Roger drove into Dorchester a few days after their return, and there heard news which brought him back home in a great hurry, his expression bleak.

Sabine sat in the drawing room, dreamily playing a new piece of music she had purchased in Weymouth, and looked round in surprise as Roger stalked into the room, still in his riding clothes, his whip in his hand.

He threw her a glance of black rage, flinging the whip down onto one of the chairs.

She stopped playing, her face anxious. "What is it? You look angry."

"Do you know who has bought Fratton Hill?" he demanded in a voice harsh with anger.

She started and remembered her own previous suspicion, which had passed out of her mind during the months past.

Roger was watching her closely, like a cat at a mouse hole. His eyes narrowed at her conscious look.

"Aye, I see you do! You plotted it together in London, I suppose? I am to be a cuckold twice over, not merely fathering another man's bastard, but standing idly by while my wife receives her lover under my very nose! Well, madam, you shall see if I am so easily cheated!"

"No, no," she protested, going white. "I did not know . . . I suspected . . . but it was only that, suspicion. I have never even mentioned it to . . ." and she stopped.

"Say his name," Roger said bitterly, and, when she was silent, said, "You cannot say it, can you? Yet you knew at once whom I meant. Deny he is your lover! Deny it!"

"I do," she said at once. "I deny it absolutely. I was foolish once, but never again. Do you think me so dishonest that I would cheat you like that?"

He stared at her in silence for a moment, then turned on his heel and stalked out.

She went to the window and stared out unseeingly. Falcon was to be so near! How could she bear it? Why had he done it? He must know how it would look. No wonder Roger was furious. He could not be blamed for suspecting her. How would she ever convince him that she had not desired this?

That night she was in bed, restless and unable to sleep, when Roger came into the room in his dressing gown and stood by her bed, staring at her.

She sat up, clutching at the sheets, her fingers trembling.

"Is something wrong?" she faltered.

He picked up the candle and held it up, studying her with glittering black eyes.

She stared back, eyes wide and frightened, her honey-colored hair falling loosely to her naked shoulders.

Without a word, he blew out the candle, placed it carefully on the little table, and turned back towards her.

She saw him looking like a falling tower as he threw himself down upon her, and then his mouth crushed down on hers, bearing her down onto the bed.

Her terrified recoil went unnoticed by him in his passion, and, since she soon forced herself to submit passively, out of a sense of duty, he was only aware of his own jealousy-driven needs until, relaxing heavily against her some time later, he felt the wetness of her face.

He sat up, cursing himself. "I'm sorry," he mumbled. "Sabine, I lost my head. Did I hurt you?

My God, child, I did not intend to hurt you. I have been drinking all evening . . . it was the wine . . ."

Without realizing it, she spoke in savage bitterness, "Your family seems to make a habit of drunken brutality!"

He winced, recognizing the reference. "He, too? Good God, but I am only fit for horsewhipping!" He lifted her hand and kissed it in repentant humility. "I would not wish to remind you of that! The last thing in the world I want to do! So he was drunk? The swine . . . And you? Why did you look at him like that in London?" His jealousy broke out in painful grief. "Why did you let me see that look of yours? You have never looked at me like that."

She lay very still, sighing. In the darkness, her face glimmered white like pearl, and he touched it again tenderly, feeling the wetness of the curved cheeks. He brushed her lashes with a finger. "Do not cry again. Did you hate it so much?" Then, hastily, "No, do not tell me. I do not want to hear. I am sorry. I shall never do so again until you give me leave."

She sighed again, more deeply, her body moving with the breath, "What right have I to deny you? You are my husband. I would not refuse you."

He groaned. "Joyless and forced? That was not what I wanted. When we made our bargain, I admit I expected a husband's rights. But my reason for marrying you was to get myself a son." He paused, stiffening. "You know I was married

once before and had no child, although my wife
in her first marriage had a son. And I have tried
elsewhere, without result. I am not able to have
children of my own. You gave me Guy, and I love
the boy. I have tried to wait patiently since his
birth. I thought you would turn to me in time.
But then I found out how you felt about Falcon,
and I have had no rest since."

She felt pity stirring in her and timidly touched
his arm. "I am sorry. I am fond of you, Roger. I
will try to love you."

He groaned again.

She sighed. "Shall we sleep now? I am tired."

He hesitated. "Shall I go back to my own room?
Would you prefer it?"

"No," she said quietly. "Things are altered now.
You might as well stay."

She slept before he did, her slender body relaxing against his, moving with her breath, unaware of her effect her nearness and soft warmth
had upon him, so that he had to clench himself
against a hunger for her which their brief, harsh
lovemaking had not assuaged.

He lay awake, listening to the regularity of her
breathing, conscious of the rounded curves of her
body lying so close to him, torn between a bitter
regret for what he had done to her and a furtive
hope for the future. Some blind instinct had made
him take her tonight. Falcon's imminent arrival
had alarmed him into a fear of losing her altogether. Now that the thing was done, he allowed
himself to hope that, by some miracle, he might
succeed with her in conceiving a child at last. His

passionate desire for a child of his own was now a dark backdrop to his every thought. His pride had been mortally wounded over the years as he lost all hope of offspring. He was the sort of man for whom manhood was necessary for self-respect, and to be incapable of fathering a child struck at the very roots of his manhood.

His knowledge of her love for Falcon did not alter his determination to keep her as his wife. Jealousy had been the final spur to a desire which had been mounting for months, and if his passionate wish for a child was his dominating emotion, his love for her came a close second by now.

He had felt forced to sleep with her tonight as though it marked her out as his property in the way that the large C burnt into the ewes which grazed his land marked them out. Now she was his in name and in reality; he felt safer. Falcon might prowl wolfishly around the borders of his estate, but he would find it well guarded now.

CHAPTER NINE

DURING the last days of May, Falcon's occupation of the Fratton Hill estate became evident. Workmen arrived and began to pull down various parts of the old house. Gossip spread through the villages like wildfire, and the servants at Ceorlbury took to whispering in corners, particularly when Falcon made no appearance there, although his presence on the hill above was well known.

From the back terrace, Sabine could see the old house, its crumbling masonry and broken roofs now in the process of coming down, and small dots of figures moving about around it. One of those dots was Falcon, she thought, feeling her pulse leap at the thought.

Roger, too, watched the proceedings from the boundaries of his own land, which he was hastily having set in order, as though he feared invasion from the neighboring estate. The keepers kept their distance from him these days. His temper was harsh and unpredictable. No one mentioned Falcon to him. They had quickly learned to avoid any mention of either Fratton Hill or its new owner.

As the months went by, the house began to grow again, but with a monolithic quality which stunned the countryside. Falcon was having Fratton Hill rebuilt like a castle, huge blocks of stone being raised where once the old red-brick walls had stood, with arched gothic windows and a high, battlemented tower to the west. Across the valley, one could see the house now, looming menacingly on the crest of the hill, with the copse which had once masked it torn up and rolling acres of grass at its foot.

The local people began to call it Falcon's Hill, and the name stuck.

Towards the end of July, Bella Amhurst arrived unannounced at Ceorlbury with Philip and caused a sensation by fainting as the carriage door was opened and having to be carried into the house by two footmen.

She was now heavily pregnant and, when revived, whispered to Roger that she had come to Ceorlbury because she felt so ill and because she wanted her child to be born in her old home.

Roger was indifferent and merely gave orders for her old rooms to be prepared for her. He had never particularly liked his sister and was now so obsessed by the darkness of his hatred for Falcon that nothing else interested him.

His relations with Sabine had not improved after his rape of her, although she attempted to smooth over any embarrassment either of them might feel. He had continued for weeks to hope that she would become pregnant, but there was no sign of it, and at last he had given up that last wild hope and relapsed into sullen misery. He got no pleasure from a passive wife, so their brief period of sharing a bed came to a sudden end.

The only living emotion inside Roger Amhurst

now was his hatred for his cousin. He fostered it
hungrily, feeding it with daily visits to his boundaries to stare up the hill at the changing walls of
Fratton's old house. The massive character of the
rebuilding seemed to tower over him, dominating
his every waking thought.

Sabine was increasingly afraid of her husband.
His had always been a silent, reserved nature. It
was becoming obsessive. His moods were violent
and strange, like freak thunderstorms striking suddenly and without warning.

She even began to fear that he was going mad.
There was a red glint in his eyes at times, a wild-
ness in his glance, which alarmed her.

She was relieved, therefore, when Bella and
Philip arrived. She still did not get on with Bella
who resented everything about her and, in her
better moods, patronized her, while in her bad
moods she came close to insulting her. Yet, at
this time, Sabine was glad of anyone who could
act as a lightning conductor.

Since Bella spent most of the day with Sabine,
Roger was forced to set some check upon his
temper, and Philip, seeing how matters stood,
kindly took it upon himself to coax Roger into a
better mood whenever he could by taking him off
to far-flung prizefights, or shooting with him over
the rough coverts on the edge of the heath land.

They saw nothing of Falcon, and this underlined his presence on the hill as nothing else could
and told them that his action in buying Fratton's
estate had been a deliberate and calculated insult
to Roger. Sabine was careful to avoid discussion

of it with Bella and Philip, afraid that Bella would repeat anything she said to Roger, with some exaggeration, and bring on one of Roger's blinding rages.

As her pregnancy advanced, Bella began to spend most of the day in her own room, sleeping or reading in bed, with a constant succession of little snacks going up to her. Sabine, at first, spent time there with her, but gradually realized that Bella did not want her and stopped the practice.

Philip continued to take Roger out of the house, especially as cubbing began in the early autumn, and Sabine felt free to resume her visits to the Dowager, of whom she had seen little since Bella's arrival.

One crisp morning in late August, she set off for the Carlew house, having seen Roger and Philip off early for Dorchester where they hoped to see a prizefight, while Bella was still sleeping.

The bronze and gold tints of the hedges and trees were lit by the early morning sunshine. The sheep had been turned into the fields to eat the stubble, and the ferns in the forest were brown and russet, whispering dryly in the little winds of autumn. She watched from her carriage window, thinking that it would soon be winter and dreading the return of short days and cold nights when she was shut into the house and unable to escape.

Lady Carlew was delighted to see her. "My dear, I have been meaning to visit you, but I have the gout. So irritating. I feel it is an unjust visitation from Providence since I have never indulged to any great extent." She eyed her foot, which, swathed in bandages, lay on a red velvet footstool. "Now my husband deserved the gout, but he escaped. There is no justice."

"Is there anything I can do to make you more comfortable, ma'am?" Sabine asked with a smile.

"Sit down and talk to me," ordered the Dowager. "I have missed you, child. My sons visit me, curse them, but they merely drive me to distraction and leave me worse than I was before. And their wives are milk-and-water females with neither brains nor bowels."

Sabine laughed. "I am sure you are very attached to them, ma'am."

"Pah! I dare say you are right, which merely goes to show that I am almost as big a fool as any of them." The Dowager gave her a sharp glance. "What is all this about Falcon? Bought Fratton's Hill and rebuilding it as the Tower of London, they tell me. Is the boy mad?"

Sabine flushed and looked down. In a colorless voice she said, "He is rebuilding Fratton's Hill, yes."

The Dowager nodded thoughtfully. "Do you see much of him?"

"No," said Sabine. "No, we do not see much of him."

"Seen anything of him at all?" demanded the Dowager, her eyes like needles.

"Nothing," Sabine said.

"I see," said the Dowager, pursing her lips. She picked up the gold-mounted cane which lay to her hand and thumped it on the floor. A nervous maid came scurrying.

"Where is that damned coffee?" the Dowager asked fiercely.

Her butler stalked in with a small table laden with coffee cups and an elegant silver coffeepot. He placed this at Sabine's elbow, ignoring the Dowager's insults with an air of stately indifference which infuriated her.

When they had sipped their coffee for a moment or two, the Dowager said, "How is Roger taking it?"

Sabine did not pretend to misunderstand her. "He is very angry," she admitted.

The Dowager watched her, one brow raised. "How angry is that?"

Sabine's lashes lifted, revealing the opalescent eyes in a condition of anxiety and pain. "I think he is going out of his mind," she burst out, then she bit her lip.

"So . . ." The Dowager stirred the rest of her coffee carefully, "Why is Falcon doing it, do you know? Revenge for losing the estate? I would not have thought him so petty. He has money enough of his own, and he could have bought any estate he took a fancy to in any part of England. Why Fratton's Hill?"

Sabine shrugged without answering.

"Roger's reaction tells us something," the Dowager continued aloud. "Whatever reason Falcon has for his actions, Roger knows it, or he would not be so angry. Has Roger spoken to you about it?"

"Not once," Sabine said, then her anxiety burst out again. "He has violent tempers all the time.

He beat in the head of one of his own dogs last
week when it got under his feet. He horsewhipped
one of the grooms until he was half-killed. He
broke half my best dinner service one evening
because a servant spilled soup on his arm, and he
slashed the portrait of Falcon's father with his
razor until it hung in ribbons from the frame."

The Dowager stared at her, openmouthed, as
panting, the girl sank back after her outburst, her
face as white as the lace on her gown.

"Good God, child, is this true? He sounds
demented. Have you sent for the doctor?"

"He would kill me if I did, I am sure of it. He
does not behave normally any more. He is unpredictable, except that I know better than to mention anything about Falcon if I do not wish to
provoke one of his terrible rages."

"Something must be behind all this," said the
Dowager, still watching her closely.

Sabine looked away again. She said nothing.

"Would it help if I brought Falcon here and
spoke to him about it? I might persuade him to go
back to London."

Sabine flushed. "Do you think you might? Oh,
ma'am, if you only could!"

"I shall," the Dowager decided. "I must go and
rest now, my dear. Why do you not walk in the
gardens until luncheon? I will see you in an hour."
She thumped on the floor, and the butler came
back with a footman, and the two men lifted her
between them, her cross voice berating them all
the while, and carried her off to bed as tenderly
as though she were a child.

Sabine put on her mantle and slipped out into the cool gardens behind the house. The air was alive with hum of bees, and the last of the roses were gently shedding scented petals on to the well-mown grass.

There was a small copse at the end of the garden. Here she wandered for a while, listening to the challenge of a blackbird perched aloft on the stable roof, answered by another from above her, their musical threats sounding oddly peaceful.

When she saw Falcon walking down the garden towards her, she was hardly surprised. A sense of inevitability stole over her. She waited for him in the green shadows, and when he joined her, they looked at each other in silence.

Shut in by the trees, they were both reminded of their first meetings at Ceorlbury in the park. Falcon leaned lazily against a silver birch, looking down at her with the hooded eyes only just open, a faint smile on his long mouth.

"I followed you here," he said at last.

"You should not have done," she said, sighing. "There is enough gossip already."

A grin twitched his lips. "Yes, there is, isn't there?" he answered solemnly.

"Why?" she asked him, in sudden anger, "why have you done it? Don't you know you are driving Roger mad? He is almost insane with jealousy. I am afraid he will kill me one day."

He stood up, his face suddenly serious, "I had not considered that. Surely not? He might kill me, but not you."

"You are as mad as he is," she said in exasperation. "Do you want to drive him out of his mind?"

"Yes," he said simply.

She stared, dumbfounded. "But . . . why? He has not harmed you."

"He owns the one thing in the world I want," he said. "He owns you. That is injury enough."

"If you really loved me," she said passionately. "You would be grateful to Roger."

"Grateful?" he echoed the word with angry disbelief. "For marrying you, for stealing you from me?"

"You did not want me then," she retorted. "You deserted me. It was Roger who saved me when I tried to kill myself . . ." then she stopped, catching her breath at the look in his eyes.

He caught her by the shoulders, breathing heavily. "Kill yourself? You did that, Sabine, for me? Did I make you so unhappy, my dearest love? Cur that I am, I did not mean to desert you. I came back for you, I swear it. I followed Philip and Bella to France, expecting to find you there, but you had gone. I was not the swine you think me."

She felt her head swim as he bent over her, his eyes burning into hers, his words tumbling out as though he needed the relief of speech.

"Why did you marry Roger?" he went on, in a half-audible voice, his face intent on hers. "If you had only waited. I would have found you and married you."

She remembered with bitterness those long, anguished days when she first realized that she was pregnant and spoke before she had considered her words. "I could not wait!"

At once she was aware that she had made a mistake. He drew back, eyes narrowing, his hands tightening on her shoulders until she winced.

"Could not wait? What do you mean?" And when, flushing, she did not reply, he shook her slightly, his lips parted in excitement. "Answer me, Sabine. Why couldn't you wait?"

She could not meet his eyes or answer. Her heart thudded in her chest making her feel quite faint.

Suddenly Falcon pulled her into his arms, his head resting on her honey-colored curls. Against her hair he whispered, "He is mine, isn't he? Guy is mine. My child. My son . . ." And the elation in his voice made her tremble until she thought she would fall.

He lifted his head after a moment and pushed up her chin so that he could look at her.

"Does Roger know?"

She did not answer.

Falcon's brows lifted quizzically, "Did he always know? Yes? Yes, I see he did. But why did he marry you, then?"

"Because he is a good man," she answered.

Falcon shook his head. "He had other reasons, didn't he, love? He disliked me, and it amused him to replace me with my own child. Did he imagine it would gall me to lose the estate? I was more angry at losing you."

"He could not have suspected that," she retorted bitterly. "Your own behavior told him the

opposite. He was magnanimous in taking your
discarded mistress as his wife."

Falcon laughed unpleasantly. "Oh, that is magnanimous! He marries you because he believes I
despise you and puts my bastard in my place as
heir to a great estate! My dear, sweet darling, do
you honestly believe Roger meant anything but
pure spite to me? He hated my guts. He thought it
would insult me to put you in such a position of
wealth and power. I was to be taught a lesson.
Come, isn't that it?"

She had to admit that he was partly right. "But
Roger has never treated me with disrespect or
unkindness," she said angrily. "He has been a
generous husband to me."

He winced. "And have you been generous to
him?" he asked dryly. Then, seeing the dark flood
of color sweep up into her cheeks, said bitterly, "I
see you have. He got the best of the bargain, didn't
he?"

"I got my life," she said. "I would be dead if it
were not for Roger. I would be dishonest if I
refused him . . . anything."

Falcon ran his hands up her arms over her
shoulders. One hand fingered her throat gently.
She looked up at him, her breath catching.

"No, Falcon . . ." she whispered, seeing the
dark intentness of his eyes, the passion of his com-
pressed lips.

But he was deaf to everything, breathing heavily, and when he bent and hungrily kissed the side
of her neck, his hand plunging into the soft curls
and wrenching them to pull her head back, she

was too dazed by her own hunger to protest at his.

He pressed her back against the silver birch, his lips traveling up her neck to her chin and then, pausing only to murmur her name, to her parted lips.

It was like suddenly plunging into icy water. The shock of his kiss made every nerve come alive and sting with pleasure. She gasped, clinging to him as to a spar, and then, giving up the unequal struggle, abandoned herself and drowned in the sweetness of aroused desire.

When he reluctantly lifted his head, she looked at him, lips parted, eyes drowsy, and smiled. All conscious thought was suspended. She was all feeling.

"My dearest," he whispered, touching her lips with one finger. "I love you, Sabine."

She held his face between her hands, smiling with sleepy content, and put her mouth on his, carefully, delicately.

And Falcon groaned and kissed her again.

"You cannot go back to Roger," he said later. "We will go away together. Europe. We will travel the world."

She was back in the real world again now, shivering and cold, her brief moments of happiness gone. "No," she said, "I cannot leave him. We must never meet again, Falcon. You must go away. Go back to London. Leave that awful house unfinished."

He laughed, kissing her nose. "My darling, you are not serious!"

"I am absolutely serious," she said, pushing

him away. "This should never have happened. It was wrong of me to let you kiss me, to let you talk to me alone here. It must never happen again. Whatever Roger's reasons for helping me, he did save my life and make me his wife. I owe him too much to hurt him."

"I cannot lose you again," he said desperately.

"We have no choice. Honor demands that we separate."

"Honor!" he said, bitterly.

She walked towards the house with him at her heels, kicking at the lawn.

"Sabine," he pleaded, "don't do this to us! Last time it was my folly that separated us. Don't do it again."

"I must," she said stubbornly. At the house, she halted and looked at him sadly. "You must go now before someone sees you."

"If I have been seen it will look very odd for me to go away without speaking to the Dowager," he said.

"I will tell her we quarreled over Fratton's Hill," she said. "She will believe me."

"You are becoming quite an accomplished little liar, aren't you?" he said.

She gave him a look of reproach and turned away. A moment later, she heard his footsteps behind her, glanced round and saw him walking round to the stables.

He had accepted her decision, then, she thought. She should be glad, yet her heart ached.

When she got back to Ceorlbury, she found the house in an uproar. Bella had been found unconscious in her bedroom, and the doctor had been hurriedly sent for from Dorchester.

Roger and Philip returned ten minutes after Sabine, having heard in Dorchester of Bella's illness. They hurried into the house to hear the news, but Sabine was unable to tell them anything.

"The doctor will not let me into the room," she told Philip. "He has been in there with her for an hour."

"Is it the baby already?" he asked anxiously.

Sabine hesitated. "I am not sure. None of the servants seem to know quite what happened. Bella was unconscious."

"Unconscious? Good God, what can be wrong?"

Sabine spread her hands in a puzzled gesture. "I do not know, Philip. She was well this morning, wasn't she?"

"She was asleep when I left," he said, and then spun on his heel as the door opened.

It was the doctor, very grave and somber. He looked at them all from beneath overhanging eyebrows. "Captain Huntley?"

"Yes," asked Philip with anxiety. "How is my wife?"

"I am dissatisfied with her," the doctor said carefully.

"Is the baby . . ." began Philip, stammering.

"It is not the baby," the doctor said, shaking his head. "But I must ask you first, has your wife been in the habit of taking laudanum?"

Philip looked surprised. "I . . . I do not know. Why? Is it not permitted? I have known many sick people to take a few drops in brandy without ill effect."

"Your wife, Captain, has taken a great deal more than that," said the other bluntly, eyeing him with severity.

"Oh," said Philip, with blank surprise. "Has it done her some harm? It has not harmed the baby?"

The doctor shrugged. "Too early to tell. Suffice it to say, your wife took enough laudanum this morning to make her unconscious for six hours and to give her a very bad shock. She must not be allowed to repeat the experience. I have removed all the laudanum from her bedroom, but I must ask you to see she does not procure any more. I suspect her to be addicted to it."

Philip seemed baffled. "Addicted? What do you mean?"

"She needs it, sir, she needs it," the doctor said sharply, as though talking to a fool.

"But if she needs it, why take it away?" asked Philip.

"Because it has a harmful effect when taken too often in too large a dose," the doctor explained irritably.

"I see," said Philip. "But I am sure she had it prescribed for her in London by her doctor there."

"I have no doubt," retorted the other. "But other men's follies are not my business. Your wife, Captain, will die if she continues to take laudanum in such large doses. A few drops now and then could do no harm to a normal person, but once someone becomes addicted to the drug, it is difficult to wean them from it."

"And the baby?" Philip asked, "Will all this have harmed the baby?"

The doctor sighed. "As I told you, I cannot say. To be frank, I do not know. But your wife will need careful nursing. She is too highly strung. She needs to be watched."

"She will be," Philip promised and, when the doctor had gone, said to Sabine that he would engage a nurse from Dorchester.

"I will be glad to nurse her," Sabine offered. "I have so little to do."

"You are too kind," he said gratefully. "I should have noticed that she was taking so much laudanum. I did notice, in fact, but I did not realize it was bad for her."

"Do not blame yourself," she urged. "You could not know."

"I must blame myself," he said somberly. "I hope to God no harm has come to the baby. It means so much to her, you know, to have a child of her own."

"I know," she said gently.

Bella was not an easy patient. She missed the soothing comfort of her daily laudanum and became irritable, feverish and spiteful when it was firmly denied to her. She seemed to blame Sabine for its loss and accused her of being cruel to her when Sabine would not bring her a fresh bottle.

In the first week of September, Bella awoke in the middle of one chilly night, complaining of indigestion, and it soon became clear that she was going into labor.

The child was born on the following afternoon. It was a girl, small-boned, dark-haired and tiny, with a frightening fragility about her.

Bella wailed her disappointment to the doctor as accusingly as though he had decided the sex of the child himself.

"Nature cannot be predicted," he said soberly. "Compose yourself, Mrs. Huntley. This agitation is not good for you. You must be calm."

She begged him for a few drops of laudanum. "Just to help me to sleep. I have not slept properly for weeks."

"I am sorry," he said, shaking his head. "It would not be good for you. You must do without it."

"Please, please," she almost screamed. "You don't know what it is like . . . how I feel . . ."

"Oh, but I do," he said, smoothing down the sheets.

"Then how can you be so cruel?" she asked. "I shall die without it . . ."

"You will live, for your baby," he said, unmoved by her shrieking.

To Philip he said that the baby was rather too small. "I am afraid she is a delicate child. But she is perfectly shaped. It is your wife who really concerns me."

"She is ill?"

"She may become so if she does not calm her nerves. She is far too volatile. Will you speak to her?"

Philip attempted to do so, but Bella was only concerned to try to procure for herself some laudanum and, when he refused to get it, would not listen to him.

She seemed to sleep badly that night, tossing restlessly, her lips dry and cracked, her voice husky.

Sabine sent for the doctor again next morning, and he came to find Bella in a high fever.

"Dear me," he said to himself, as he stood by the bed with one hand on Bella's wrist.

"She has birth fever," Sabine said quietly to him.

He looked sharply at her and smiled, for the first time since he had entered the house.

"You are a good little nurse, Mrs. Amhurst. Yes, she has the birth fever. We must try to bring the fever down. Give her plenty to drink. Nothing to eat. And," he sighed, and held out a tiny bottle, "two drops of this twice a day. Morning and night."

She took it, frowning. "What is it?"

He smiled again, dryly, "You have guessed, I think. I am defeated. She must have it to calm her. When she is perfectly well, we will wean her from it again."

Sabine sighed, but took the bottle to Bella, whose glazed eyes shone at the sight of it.

"Laudanum," she said feverishly. "Now I shall sleep. I was right. I knew what I needed. . . ."

But, it seemed, the laudanum came too late to save her life. The fever mounted rapidly, and, twenty-four hours later, Bella died.

"I am sorry," the doctor said to Philip, who sat at the bedside with his head in his hands.

"Was it the laudanum?" Sabine asked him.

He shook his head. "Birth fever is frequent in older mothers. It is less usual in houses as this where the bed linen is clean and every effort is made to keep the mother healthy, but it still happens. I could do nothing. The laudanum was a separate issue, you understand." He let his shoulders droop. "At least the child is doing well. You have a good wet nurse?"

Sabine nodded. "One of our cottagers who lately lost her own child."

"Good, good. If you need me, I will come at once." He nodded to her and left.

Roger took Philip down to the gun room to drown his sorrows while Sabine and Marette watched with Bella's body. The house seemed silent and empty, as though everyone walked on tiptoe in the presence of death.

"She knew what came to her," Marette said darkly. "She comes home to die, not for the child to be born. It is in her face when she steps out of the carriage that first day. She knew."

Sabine did not answer. It seemed to her tragic that no one, even here, lamented Bella's death with any depth. Even Philip was merely conscience-stricken and pitiful. He had not loved her. Roger, too, was merely sorry for his sister. They had never been very close. In all that house, there was no living soul to mourn her with love.

It was a pathetic end.

CHAPTER TEN

AT Bella's funeral, Roger was so drunk that Philip had to stand close to him to support him throughout the long service, and the scandalized congregation watched with amazement as Roger tripped when he tried to lift his corner of the coffin and fell headlong into the aisle where he lay laughing while Philip tried to help him up.

Sabine was bitterly conscious of the whispers and the sidelong glances at herself. All Roger's misdeeds were laid at her door. He had always drunk heavily, but now he was on the point of dementia, and they blamed her.

Scarlet-faced, Philip guided Roger back into place. "Old Philip. Old friend," Roger thanked him solemnly. "Good fellow, Philip." The parson waited, stiff with outrage, and the other men strained to lift the coffin, always aware of Roger's smothered snorts as his legs wavered beneath him.

Falcon, Mrs. Amhurst and Fanny, all in black, were discreetly seated at the back of the church, having refused to join the family in the Amhurst pew. Sabine had been aware of their presence at once and had wondered how Falcon had the courage to come into Roger's sight even on such an occasion. The church had run with comment as the three entered and took their places so far from the family pew.

Only the violence of Roger's hatred for Falcon could explain the fact that he had not invited them to the funeral. Yet here they were, uninvited.

She hoped Roger would not notice them.

The burial proceeded at a more dignified rate for a while, and when Bella had been consigned to the bosom of her ancestors, the mourners emerged into the sunlight outside.

The trees were stripping for winter. The churchyard was full of crisp golden leaves, blown about by a brisk wind, filling up all the crevices between the graves, obscuring the sunken memorials to earlier Amhursts, whispering over the paving stones of the path.

Roger was absurdly maudlin now, his arm thrown about Philip's neck, sobbing out his regrets for his sister.

"I never liked her, d'y'know, Philip? Tha' was wicked. Very wicked. I should have liked her. She was my sister, after all. I should have cher . . . cher . . . cherished her." He suddenly laughed, to the scandal of the silent, watching congregation, "Cherished her like a snake in my bosom. She said that to me about Sabine . . . my wife! Insolent bitch! My sister was a bitch!" Then he drew a thickened breath and his brief anger passed back into a sob, "Poor Bella! Mustn't say that. Dead, dead, dead. Poor old bitch!"

Philip steered him towards the waiting carriages. Roger lifted his black hat to the watching crowd, sneering drunkenly.

"Wha' you staring at, damn you? This is a funeral not a fair. Get out, the lot o' you . . ." And ran stumblingly at the nearest little group, swinging his hat in his hand.

Philip caught him, sweating miserably, and led him back to the carriages.

Sabine whispered to Falcon, meeting him in the churchyard. "Please, please do not let him see you! He will kill you."

He shrugged without answering, and she lifted her skirts and hurried after her husband and Philip who were just climbing into the leading carriage.

The carriage started off at once, sending Roger flying onto Sabine's lap, where he laughed foolishly, scrambling up to kiss her face.

Over his head, her eyes met Philip's, and they looked at each other in silence.

Roger was almost asleep when they arrived at the house. He woke with a start and allowed them to lead him indoors without any further trouble.

Sabine made no attempt to stop him drinking the rest of a bottle of port, and, when he fell senseless onto the sofa, Philip carried him upstairs with the aid of the butler.

The other guests left almost immediately in a frozen silence, and Sabine sank down on a chair, wondering what was to become of them.

Philip attempted to leave Ceorlbury next day, pleading a desire to remove his unwelcome presence from Roger's remembrance, but Sabine begged him to stay.

"I have no place here now," he said heavily. "Bella is dead. It is all over."

"Please," she said. "Roger likes you. He needs you, Philip. He must be persuaded to stop drinking, but I dare not ask him."

"Are you very frightened, Sabine?" he asked gently, his fair face full of kindness and concern.

"I am terrified," she admitted in a quiet tone. "I wake up each morning wondering what will happen during the day, and I go to bed each evening wondering . . ." she stopped, flushing. "Yes, Philip," she went on, "I am frightened."

He watched her thoughtfully. "For yourself, or of something else? Do you think he may harm you?"

"More that he may harm himself or someone else," she said.

"Falcon?" he suggested.

She flushed again. "Falcon," she agreed very quietly.

"He hates the very sound of his name, doesn't he? What is Falcon playing at up there on the hill?"

"He is tormenting Roger," she said unhappily. "He wants to make him angry."

"He is succeeding," he said grimly. "It must be stopped."

"I have tried," she confessed with some embarrassment. "I was frank with him. But he has not gone. The house is almost finished now. The very sight of it drives Roger wild. Sooner or later, he will do something terrible to Falcon."

"Perhaps Falcon does not realize how far he is driving Roger mad," Philip suggested.

"He knows," she said angrily. "I think he wants

Roger to try to kill him. It is as if they both need to bring the thing to some climax."

"A trial of strength? Yes, that may be it. I will go and see Falcon myself and see what I can do." Philip stood up. "I . . . I cannot go yet, though."

She looked puzzled. "Why not?"

He flushed. "Fanny is there, isn't she? I cannot meet her so soon . . . it would not be right. . . ."

Sabine smiled at him and pressed his hand. "Poor Philip. I hope it will all come right for you at last. You are so kind and good."

He laughed. "Only you could say that, Sabine, out of your sweetness of heart. I am a mercenary, weak-minded wretch, but I do love Fanny very deeply. I don't deserve to be happy, but I cannot help hoping that I may be one day."

The baby was christened some weeks later, very quietly, and given its mother's name, Arabella.

Roger was still dependent upon Philip's company, and would not hear of his leaving Ceorlbury. The new baby, he announced, should be brought up with Guy on the estate.

"They will be company for each other," he told Sabine, in one of his sober moments. There were still times when he was gentle and good-humored towards her, but these came in rare flashes and could not be relied upon.

He drank now from first thing in the morning as though he could not stand his own thoughts when he was sober, and he never went up to the nursery to see Guy whose very name seemed to bring on a fierce seizure of wrath. Sabine dreaded the possibility of Roger's so losing his temper that he would publicly proclaim the fact that Guy was not his own son but Falcon's.

One evening he came to her room, almost blindly drunk, and made violent advances to her only to collapse in a stupor on the floor within five minutes. Relieved, yet sick, she lifted him onto her own bed and left him there in his boots and coat to sleep it off, while she slept on his bed.

Marette was grim in the morning as she dressed her mistress. Roger stumbled to his feet, white-faced and sullen, and vanished downstairs without a word.

"You must suffer this!" Marette exploded, her heavy face twisted with hatred of Roger.

"Ssssh . . ." Sabine ordered. "He is a good man. He is sick."

Marette laughed. "Oh, yes, we all know with what he is sick! He is a pig, that one."

"Marette!" Sabine cut in angrily. "Never say so again! You are wrong . . . you do not understand. He has much to try him."

"The other one? Yes?" Marette smiled grimly at Sabine's surprise. "You think I do not know? I know you, madame. And I have heard him, the pig, talking to himself in the night when he is the most drunk. He talks of this other, with hatred, yes? He would kill him. Why, what does he expect, an old man like him marrying a beautiful young girl like you? It is the way of the world."

"Oh, Marette," Sabine sighed wearily, "please, do not talk like that. You make me unhappy. You do not understand." She stood up and walked to the window. "Is there much gossip about this?"

"The other servants do not seem to know, although they do know the master hates his cousin. They do not know what I know, if that is what you mean."

Sabine nodded. "Then never speak of it again. Please. Will you promise?"

Marette shrugged. "Very well. As you please." But she looked sidelong at her mistress, with a little smile. "He is handsome, the other one. A man to love, yes?"

Sabine left the room without answering. She found Philip and asked him to go up to Falcon's Hill, as it was now called by everyone, and beg Falcon to go away, at least for a while.

"For my sake," she added quietly.

"I am to say that?" Philip asked with a very serious look.

She nodded.

"Very well," Philip nodded, and went that day.

Sabine was on tenterhooks until he returned, and when she heard his step in the hall, she sat up, eyes dilating, and watched the door intently.

He came in, looking very uneasy, and crossed the room to her without speaking.

"Well?" she asked dryly.

"I saw him," he began in a careful tone. He paused, "Roger is out?"

"Yes, yes, what did he say? Will he go?"

"He makes conditions," Philip said flatly.

"Conditions? What conditions?"

"He wishes to see you before he leaves. If you will meet him just once, he swears he will go away for a year at least." Philip kept his eyes on the window, never looking at her face, his tone almost casual.

"Oh," she said, biting her lip.

There was a long pause. Then she asked, "What did you say to him then?"

"I said I would give you that message," Philip answered in the same light tone.

"He must be mad to ask it," she said. "If Roger found out . . . what good will it serve, anyway? I will not do it. I cannot do it."

Philip did not speak.

"Philip," she said desperately, "I am too much afraid to do it!"

Philip looked at her then, kindly. "I said as much to Falcon. I told him how frightened you were. It was then that he said he would go under this condition."

She stood up and walked about the room, nervously twisting her hands together.

"He must go, he must. But how can I meet him? Why does he ask me to? He knows how I feel . . ." she stopped, shivering. "I am so frightened that I cannot think properly."

"Sleep on it," Philip advised. "I will go back tomorrow and see if I can talk Falcon out of this idea of meeting you."

"Will you? Oh, do, Philip, do." She came to him and held his hand like a drowning creature, her eyes turned up to him, full of tears.

There was a crash behind them, and Roger halted on the threshold, glaring. "What's this, damn you? Making love to my wife? You little damned cur, I'll kill you . . ." He rushed out

again, and they heard him banging about somewhere, his voice raised in an angry tirade.

"Oh, what shall we do, Philip?" moaned Sabine,
clinging to him.

He put her aside gently. "I will go and calm
him down," he said. "He will usually listen to me."

But before he reached the door Roger appeared
holding a pistol in each hand, his face twisted
with black rage.

Philip froze in his tracks. Quietly he said,
"Roger, you are quite out in your suspicions. How
can you think I would do such a thing to you, old
fellow?"

Sabine put her trembling hands over her mouth
to stop herself from screaming.

Red-eyed and glaring like a mad dog, Roger
choked out words, "You've been mighty friendly
with her all along. I must have been blind. Once a
whore, always a whore. But she is mine, and I
won't have other men nosing round her . . ." He
leveled the pistol in his right hand with a wavering
grasp, sweat breaking out on his forehead and
trickling down into his dilated eyes.

Philip began to walk very slowly, his eyes fixed
on Roger's with a calm, steady gaze. "You are
wrong. I respect you too much. I like you, Roger.
You are my friend." He spoke carefully, as to a
madman.

Roger's hands shook, but with a muttered oath
he pulled back the hammer, and there was a crash
in the silent room which brought Sabine's heart
into her mouth. A scream left her throat and was

choked back. She leapt forward and caught Philip as he fell, his left sleeve staining bright red.

Roger stared, as if not believing what he saw, then he flung the pistols down on the floor and stumbled out of the room, sobbing harshly.

The servants crowded into the doorway, staring. She saw Jabez Starling among them and told him to run after Roger. "Stop him and bring him back. He is ill."

"What about Captain Huntley?" Jabez asked.

"Send for the doctor and bring me some warm water and my workbasket," she ordered.

Philip was very white. She could see that he was in considerable pain, and when she helped him to the sofa, he fainted, half on and half off, and had to be lifted up onto the cushions.

The workbasket was brought. She got her scissors and cut free the bottom of the sleeve, laying bare the wound. Blood streamed down his arm and fell onto the silk cushions of the sofa.

"I am sorry," he gasped, trying to smile, as he saw the mess the blood made.

She felt a hysterical desire to laugh. "It doesn't matter a jot," she told him, shuddering.

When the water came, she gently washed away the blood and saw that the wound was a deep one, singed and torn flesh laid bare to the bone.

She winced at his pain and made him drink a large glass of brandy, after which he lay back more easily, with his eyes closed.

The hour before the doctor came was the longest of her life. Jabez came back to say that Roger had disappeared and could not be found. She thanked him and dismissed him. She heard voices in the hall and, going to the window, saw that some of the men were standing outside with loaded pistols.

"What is it?" Philip whispered.

She told him uncertainly what she had seen.

"Ah," he whispered. "They are afraid he may be armed still. If he comes back, I hope he is saner. They may shoot him."

"They would not!" she protested, and went out of the room. Jabez stood in the hall with the butler. They looked at her in silence.

Although the villagers and many of their neighbors blamed Sabine for Roger's drunkenness, the servants, who saw her daily, did not. Roger had always drunk heavily, long before he met her, and her gentleness and kindness to all at Ceorlbury had brought her a popularity which no gossip could kill. Their sympathies were with their mistress, especially since they were, of all people, aware that there had never been anything but friendship between her and Philip.

Philip was popular, too, for his good temper and quietness, and the fact that Roger had shot him made the servants very uneasy. They had valued Philip as the last person capable of bringing out Roger's old good humor. If he had turned on Philip, he was in a very dangerous state of mind, and they were all afraid that next time it would be themselves. His vicious treatment of several of the servants had already frightened them. Now they were seriously alarmed.

"Put away those pistols," Sabine ordered.

Jabez looked at the butler, who shook his head.

"I am sorry, ma'am," said Jabez sturdily. "We've the right to defend ourselves, I think. Squire's run mad. We all know that. No man cares to be shot down like a dog without at least trying to protect himself."

"He would not shoot you," she protested. "But if he sees you all out there with guns, he may really go mad."

"I'm sorry, ma'am," Jabez returned, shrugging.

"Jabez," she pleaded, but to no avail. Their faces were stubborn.

"Have you no notion where he has gone?" she asked, after a moment.

Jabez hesitated. "Towards the old copse," he said after a moment.

"On foot?"

"On horseback," he said, paused, and added, "armed. He took an old pistol from the stable, which Jack Fowler keeps for scaring off foxes from the hen house."

She shuddered. "Where will he go, do you think?"

Jabez shrugged. "Up Fratton Hill, maybe," he said casually, and their eyes met.

Her hand went to her mouth. "Oh." She hesitated, torn between fear and discretion.

Then she made up her mind. "Jabez, send someone up to the new house. Warn them there that your master is . . ." she paused, wondering how to phrase it, but Jabez needed no second telling.

"Aye," he said stalwartly, "I'll send Jack Fowler. He knows Master Falcon well from the old days when he was a lad. He will know what to say."

She nodded and went back into the drawing room. Philip was in a faint again, his arm hanging loose over the edge of the sofa. She sat down and watched his face, wondering what Roger was doing and whether he was making for Falcon's Hill with the intention of killing Falcon.

She was to blame for all this. Had she been able to see into the future on that far-off evening, she would have refused Roger's offer of marriage and gone straight back into the water to die. She had brought disaster to Ceorlbury without meaning to do so.

If Roger kills Falcon, she thought with a cold feeling about her heart, I shall want to die. What will there be left to live for?

CHAPTER ELEVEN

THE doctor came and, without comment, attended to Philip's wound, his face severe, and his manner reserved. Sabine held the bowl of water he required, averting her eyes as the water turned bright red, and winced at every movement, feeling Philip's pain as though it were her own. When it was all over, she was as white as he, and the doctor observed her thoughtfully.

"You have borne a great deal recently, Mrs. Amhurst. I think you need to rest. I will give you something to calm your nerves."

"No," she said at once, shaking her head, "thank you, but that is out of the question."

He looked down his nose, his expression offended. "I think you would be wise to do as I suggest."

"I must be here, in case . . ." she broke off, bit her lip, and resumed, "I must be here, downstairs. I cannot sleep."

He raised his brows curiously, but made no further remark. "Captain Huntley will do, now. I will give you some medicine for him—you will permit that, I presume?" he said sarcastically. "And he must be allowed to sleep, so we will have him carried to his room. Rest is essential if blood poisoning is not to set in. . . ."

She was grateful that he had asked no questions

and thanked him with great warmth before he left. Jabez stood in the hall, his face wooden, watching as she said goodbye to the doctor. When the door had shut, she turned and looked a question.

He shook his head silently.

She sighed and went back to the drawing room, wondering why Jabez stood in the hall like that and why he was not out with the others searching for Roger.

She would have been surprised to find out that Jabez was there to protect her from her husband. Hidden in the angle of the staircase was a gun, ready loaded, should Roger return to the house unseen by the watchers outside. Jabez was leaving nothing to chance.

Sabine sat watching the clock, its hand jerking noisily around its face. The minutes flicked past. Then the hours. Time stretched out before her in a barren waste, and her mind was consumed with a delirious anxiety.

Then a step in the hall made her stiffen. She heard Jabez, his voice sounding strange, then another voice which brought her heart up into her mouth.

The door opened. She sat where she was, a hand on each arm of her chair, looking at Falcon.

He closed the door and was across the room, kneeling beside her chair, his face anxious and self-reproachful.

"This is all my fault," he said. "Sabine, are you unharmed? They say Philip has been shot. Did he hurt you, too?"

"Are you insane, to come here of all places? Roger's out with his gun, looking for you. Why

have you come here? This is the very last place.
. . . He will kill us both."

He shook his head. "This house is like a be-
sieged town. There are men everywhere, with
guns, watching for him. I was stopped fifty times
or so, I swear." He lifted her hand and kissed it
soberly. "I had to come, my darling. Could I leave
you to face this alone when it is all my fault?"

"It would have been better if you had," she
said, her nerves jumping at every little sound.

"Tell me what happened. Why did he turn on
Philip?"

She shrugged. "He is no longer rational enough
for me to guess."

Falcon drew back and looked at her, his blue
eyes quizzical, "If I did not know you and Philip
very well, my dearest, I would suspect you of eva-
sion." He grinned at her. "Come, tell me what
happened."

She knew that hot color had mounted into her
cheeks. "He . . . he made wild accusations . . ."
she stammered, looking away.

"Of you and Philip?" Falcon made a dry sound
of amusement. "I hope that is not so—it would
ruin a long and happy friendship." He looked
teasingly at her, "You are not falling in love with
Philip, my dear?"

She was angry and showed it. "You are as
ridiculous as Roger! It was so silly. Philip was
comforting me, that is all. Roger saw him holding
my hand and . . ."

"Philip is a lucky man!" he commented. "So
Roger jumped to conclusions and shot him?" He

became serious again. "But Philip is not badly hurt? It was only a flesh wound?"

"In the shoulder," she said, "just above the arm. I had to cut away his sleeve. There was blood everywhere." She swallowed, shuddering. "It was horrible . . ."

"Flesh wounds always bleed a good deal," he said lightly. "Roger did not threaten you, then?"

"No," she said. "No, he looked surprised when Philip fell, and he ran out of the room. But, Falcon, they say he made towards your new house. He may have seen you on your way here. He may have followed you."

He shrugged. "I hope he has, so that the men outside can catch him. We cannot have a lunatic with a loaded gun holding the countryside to ransom."

She shivered. "It is so terrifying to think of him out there, somewhere, waiting. . . ."

There was the sound of a shot out in the park, and she gave a cry of horror and leapt to her feet. Falcon was already at the window when she stumbled to it, but he turned as she came up and put an arm about her, comfortingly.

"It was a mistake. Don't shake so, my darling. One of the keepers saw something move over there, see? But he only shot one of Roger's deer. They are so nervous that they will shoot anything that moves."

"Oh, God," she moaned, her teeth chattering.

He led her back to the sofa. "You must not let yourself get into a state of terror like this. Let me pour you a glass of brandy. It will calm you."

She made no demur, and when he brought her

the brandy, drank it, grimacing, and was grateful for the warmth it engendered.

"Falcon, they must not kill Roger. Tell Jabez. They must not shoot him unless he shoots at them. He may be out there, frightened, wondering what to do. Oh, what have I done? It is all my fault. I should never have married him. I have brought all this on us. But they must not kill him."

"I'll tell him," Falcon said, soothingly, and went out into the hall.

She heard the murmur of their voices, then Falcon came back, frowning.

"Did Jabez promise?" she asked anxiously.

Falcon shrugged. "He says the men are not fools. They will not shoot to kill and will only shoot if they have to in self-defense."

She wrapped her arms around herself and rocked to and fro like a child. "This waiting is killing me. If only we knew what he was doing. . . ."

Falcon sat down in a chair, stretching out his long legs, "Well, let us pass the time with talking. You know that my mother and sister have returned from the West Indies?"

She gave a stiff smile. "Yes, I . . . I saw them. Did they enjoy their visit?"

"Very much it appears, but they found it rather too hot. They only arrived back in England a week before Bella's funeral. I was extremely sorry to hear of her death, by the way. It was very unexpected and sudden."

She felt as though she were caught in a nightmare, trapped in unreality. They talked politely, as though nothing were happening that was abnormal or frightening. Falcon appeared perfectly calm, his manner courteous and friendly. Yet outside Roger roamed with murder in his heart.

"I suppose we should not be precipitate," Falcon said. "But Bella's death does make my sister's future a little happier. It will take time, of course. One does not lightly turn out of the conventional path. But in a year or so . . . Will you wish them happy, Sabine? You will not think it wrong in Philip and Fanny to claim their happiness?"

She shook her head. "Of course not. But it is too soon after Bella's death to discuss it. . . ."

He inclined his head. "You are right. Let us change the subject. How is Guy?" And his smile was swift, secret, intimate.

She flushed, lowering her eyes. "He is well."

Falcon sat up. "He is safe, isn't he? Roger could not get up there without being seen?"

"I have been to the nursery," she said. "His nurse has locked the door, on my instructions, and there is no other way to get into the room. The door would have to be broken down, and we should all hear that."

He relaxed, sighing. "I am relieved to hear it."

There was silence. Then he began to talk again, of the work of redecorating his new house, which was proceeding very well, it seemed. She sat, half-listening, half-abstracted. Then she heard a strange sound out in the hall. A muffled snort, a thud and a dragging movement.

Falcon was on his feet, his muscles tensed. He pushed Sabine to one side, his eyes fixed on the door, and hissed, "Get behind the sofa . . ."

She hardly heard him, so intent was she on the slowly opening door.

As Roger came into the room, they both saw Jabez lying on his face in the hall in a pathetic crumpled heap.

"Oh, you have killed Jabez," Sabine cried, without thinking, running forward towards the hall.

Roger caught her as she ran and held her, his engorged face contorted with hatred. Over her head, his eyes flashed hatred at Falcon.

He leveled his pistol, eyes fixed. Sabine struggled in his grip and succeeded in knocking the pistol upwards. It went off with a sound which made her cringe, and white plaster showered down on them from the ceiling. Roger was startled. He automatically brushed at his face, where the dust lay in thick flakes.

Falcon launched himself forward, and the two men fell with a heavy sound and began rolling about, their arms flailing. Sabine ran around like a frightened little animal, trying to think what to do but unable to distinguish them from each other as the dark heads moved from side to side, ducking and rearing.

She heard the sound of shouting outside and running feet, then the men were in the hall and had found Jabez. They came into the room, pistols cocked, and stood, watching the fight.

"Stop them, stop them," she implored, but, having realized that neither was armed, they did nothing but watch, their eyes interested.

Sabine saw she would get no help there. She looked about and picked up a blue and white porcelain vase. She brought it down unflinchingly upon one of the heads and saw, with a pang, that she had chosen Falcon.

His head slumped. Roger pushed him off and stood up. With a savagely contorted expression, he kicked him in the ribs before Sabine ran and seized his arm.

"No, no, you must not—Oh, Roger, do not!"

He looked down at her, the massive head lowered, like that of a bull about to charge. His reddened eyes were full of angry misery. He shook his head as if fly-beset, and then looked at the watching men, silently waiting, their pistols still held leveled at him.

Shaking her off, he walked slowly towards them, and they as slowly backed, their eyes intent on his advancing figure. With a darting movement, Roger suddenly snatched a pistol from the nearest man, who fumbled desperately at it as he did so, and Jack Fowler, the head keeper, said sharply: "Squire, throw it down . . . or we shoot! We dunnot want to harm 'ee but if we must we shall. . . ."

Roger laughed arrogantly and put the pistol into his mouth. The men froze. Sabine screamed. Then there was the heavy explosion, and Roger fell forward on his face.

Sabine awoke in a gray dawn light a week later and watched the cold room slowly filling with wintry sunshine. Marette came in to draw back the curtains and looked quickly at her.

"Marette," she said, "pack some clothes. We are going to France."

The maid's heavy face lit up. "Very good, madame," she said, beaming, "and the child?"

"We shall take him with us, of course," Sabine said, with a weary gesture. She was in a state of complete exhaustion, both mental and physical, and she needed to get away from Ceorlbury. She never wished to see the house again.

"And . . . M'sieur Falcon?" asked Marette slyly, glancing at her.

Sabine shivered. "No, we go at once. I do not want him to know where I am."

Since Roger's funeral, the house had been silent and empty as though all human life had deserted it. The scandal of his suicide had made Sabine an outcast in the country. She was blamed for his drunken decline and for his final act of madness. No one but the Dowager had called, and Sabine had refused to see her, pleading illness. She had remained in her own room, isolated, brooding, self-reproachful, but now she had come to a decision. She would leave here for good. Guy would be brought up elsewhere. They would never return.

Falcon could inherit Ceorlbury as he should have done, and she would learn to forget him.

Having made her decision, she put it into immediate operation. The carriage came round at noon. The trunks were put on top, and the three climbed in: Sabine with Guy dancing on her lap, Marette frowning darkly as she watched her mistress. Jabez stood at the window of the carriage and looked at them all with a smile of regret. Roger had merely stunned him when he struck him on the back of the head with his pistol, but the blow had left him pale and hollow-eyed, with constant headaches.

"I am sorry you mean to leave us," he said gently. "People have short memories, you know. You would be wiser to stay."

She shook her head. "I cannot. Goodbye, Jabez. Thank you for all you have done for me."

He shrugged, smiled, and the carriage drew away.

Jabez looked up at the hillside above the house. He had sent Falcon a message when Sabine gave orders for the carriage to be brought round that morning, and had been hourly expecting to see Falcon galloping down the hill towards them. But there was no sign of him. Was he happy, then, to see her leave? Had Jabez misread his mind? Shrugging, he went back into the house. He had done all he could for her. It was up to Falcon now.

Falcon, meanwhile, was in Dorchester with Philip, where they had been since early morning. They left for Falcon's Hill after luncheon and rode back easily through the bare countryside, talking rarely.

Philip had moved up to Falcon's Hill at Falcon's suggestion after Roger's death and was much improved in health. His flesh wound still troubled him, but the expected fever had not materialized, and he could ride well enough with his arm in a sling. Mrs. Amhurst and Fanny had withdrawn to London to escape the county gossips, so the two men had plenty of time on their hands.

When they reached the new house, they were met with Jabez's letter. Falcon broke the seal casually and read it, then gave an exclamation of shocked disbelief.

"What is it?" asked Philip, and Falcon thrust it into his hand as he tore out of the house towards the stables. Philip read it, shook his head in dismay, but did not follow his friend. He would make

a poor third in that discussion, he decided, and
retired to the parlor to read.

On reaching Ceorlbury, Falcon found that he
had missed the carriage by a full two hours, and,
after a hurried consultation with Jabez as to desti-
nation, he returned to his home to pack some
things before setting out again.

He finally caught up with them in Southampton
at a small inn, and Sabine looked round in dismay
as she heard his voice in the passage outside the
parlor where she sat.

Falcon came in, stripping off his gloves, his
greatcoat flapped open. His face glowed from his
ride, and he looked tired and cold.

She sat alone, a book on her lap, dressed all in
black. Falcon stood looking at her, a small smile
on his lips. They had not seen each other since the
day of Roger's suicide.

"Did you think I would let you go like this?"
he asked casually, taking off his greatcoat and
dropping it on a chair.

She did not reply, and he waited, stretching his
frozen hands towards the fire which leapt and spat
in the great hearth.

Then he dropped down on one knee and put
both hands over hers, smiling at her in that old
intimate way which made her heart, even now,
turn over.

"I agree that you must go away," he said. "For
a year if you wish, my love. But then you will
come back to me."

"No," she said, in a voice rusty and worn.

His features glowed with passionate determination. "Yes," he repeated.

"I cannot ever see you again," she said.

"Any guilt in this is mine," he interrupted her quickly. "Had I not deserted you, none of it would have happened. But I was weak and stupid, not deliberately wicked. Are we to ruin the rest of our lives for my brief moments of folly? I love you. I am sure that you love me. What else matters?"

"Roger is dead because of me," she said miserably, turning her eyes away from the dark face so close to hers. She could not bear to see him. It hurt too much.

"Bella is dead because of Philip, but he is too sensible to wreck his life because of it."

"That is different. She died in childbed."

"She would not have done had she never married Philip," he said.

"It is not the same," she repeated, putting her hands to her head. "Don't, please don't, Falcon. I cannot think properly. I am so tired. Leave me alone, please. I cannot stand much more."

"Sabine," he whispered, bending closer, but she gave a stifled cry and pushed him away.

Marette was suddenly in the room, a whirling dark-faced fury. "You must go, m'sieur," she ordered, tapping him on the shoulder. Her rigidly angry glance made him flush. "She has no strength to bear more. Do as she says. Leave her."

He stood up, hesitated, then walked to the door. Marette followed him.

In the passage outside, she whispered, "Go now, m'sieur, and do not fear. I will stay with her, and I will write to you now and then to let you know how it is with her. But for the present, she is too weak to bear any more burdens. She needs to forget. Be wise. Leave her time to put those black memories behind her."

He stared into her heavy features. "You swear you will write to me? Let me know where she is and how she is?"

"I swear. For the present, she intends to go to Brittany. But we may move on elsewhere. I will keep you *au fait* with her movements."

He nodded. "Very well. I must trust you, I suppose." He put some money into her hands. "This is for your postal dues. Do not forget." Then he was gone.

Marette went back to her mistress and found her sobbing uncontrollably in the chair. She knelt and embraced her roughly, her hand against her curly head. "Sssh . . . *restez tranquille ma chere.* He has gone."

Sabine's sobs redoubled, and she shook with grief. Over her bent head, Marette smiled.

She kept her word. Every few weeks, a letter arrived from her with news of Sabine, and Falcon lived on them from day to day, reading and re-reading them with obsessive pleasure. He had little images of Sabine and Guy in tiny French villages, living among the peasants in a simple way, wearing the black which is so familiar to the French women. Spring came and wore away into full, high summer. Marette wrote of moving into the mountains to leave behind the slow hot days of the French interior, and then wrote again when they moved down for the grape harvest. Now he had a picture of Sabine watching the grape treading, beginning to laugh again, her skin a golden brown, her eyes healthy and alive once more.

The trio moved to Paris for the autumn, and Marette casually mentioned a French admirer, a handsome young Frenchman with a fine estate in the Auvergne. Falcon's lips tightened as he read Marette's glowing phrases of admiration for this unknown gentleman.

"It seems to me to be time for me to do something," he said to Philip.

Philip read the offending epistle, smiled and said, "No, I should wait a while longer, Falcon. It is still a little soon."

"I do not want to lose her again," Falcon said.

Philip shook his head, laughing, "You know her better than that."

"It would suit Marette admirably to have her settle in France," Falcon snapped.

"Marette?" repeated Philip, with bewilderment. "She is only her maid, my dear Falcon."

"She has great influence with her," Falcon said with some foreboding.

Philip laughed again. "You are looking for excuses, Falcon."

They exchanged wry looks, and Falcon grinned self-deprecatingly. "I am, you are right. It seems more than a year since I last saw her. By the way, my dear fellow, it is time I invited my mother and sister to spend a few weeks here, isn't it?"

Philip flushed. "Oh . . . well, of course, that is your own affair."

"Of course," Falcon agreed blandly. "My

mother wrote to me yesterday of a famous match she is trying to make for Fanny. With Lord St. Clair Wringham."

Philip looked suddenly white. "He is fifty, if he is a day! She cannot be serious."

"Or, she thinks, Pascal Hendsham might suit. He is only twenty-four and has a vast fortune, but he is a trifle wild and is known to have kept three mistresses at a time without any loss of stamina. Quite a feat! Now he would fit quite well into our family, don't you think?"

Philip met the mocking eyes without blanching. "I can hardly comment," he said stiffly.

"Fanny might be a trifle unhappy with either," Falcon said. "Oh, come, my dear Philip, pluck up your spirits. Fanny has waited long enough to be happy. I will not allow you to trifle with her affections any longer. The betrothal shall be announced next month. It is, after all, more than a year since Bella died. Convention has been satisfied. And your little girl needs a mother."

Philip hesitated. "I do not know that Fanny will accept me," he said.

Falcon grinned at him. "And I do not know if I can eat my dinner today, but I intend to have a stab at doing so!"

Philip laughed. "Very well. I will ask her."

"You sound so grudging," Falcon said mockingly.

Philip looked very seriously at him. "You know how I feel. I am only afraid she cannot entirely respond."

"If I have learned anything in the last few years,

Philip," Falcon told him, "it is that love must not be trifled with. If I had had the courage of my convictions when I first met Sabine, I would have married her at once. I was afraid to do so, and I have lived to regret it bitterly. Take my advice. Seize love and enjoy it while you can."

Fanny left Philip in no doubt as to her feelings from the first day of her arrival. Her shyness had not abated, but the first look from those gentle, confiding eyes told him all that he wanted to know. Within a week, they were betrothed, and Mrs. Amhurst accepted the news with resignation. She was half-relieved to have Fanny safely off her hands. She had begun to think she would never contrive to do it.

Having settled his sister's happiness, Falcon packed his bags and left for France with high hopes of achieving the same end for himself.

He arrived in Paris one chilly November evening and hurried at once to the hotel from where Marette had last written, only to discover that the birds had flown. He discovered, however, that they were still in Paris, but on a visit to a French family whose name he recognized as that of the wealthy, handsome young gentleman of whom Marette had written so glowingly.

In a terrified passion of jealousy, Falcon made his way to the address. A footman opened the door, looked down his long nose and denied him admittance. The family were at dinner. Falcon retreated.

He remained outside, watching the candle glow in the windows, the shadow show of movement which spoke of people walking about talking in a long salon.

The front door opened. Linkboys and carriages sprung up from nowhere. There was the sound of gay voices, the rustle of silks and much coming and going.

Falcon remained in the shadows, watching with fixed gaze. Suddenly he saw her, slender, honey-hair elaborately dressed, her shoulders bare but the opal necklace around her throat. She was being assisted into a carriage by a young man whose slim good looks made Falcon's fists clench at his sides. She paused, smiling up at her escort, and then she was out of sight.

As they drove away, he thought he heard her laughter from within the carriage, and his lips drew back in a snarl.

Had he waited too long? Had she forgotten him already? She had looked so gay and happy. Her face, which had lost so much flesh over the last months before Roger's death, had filled out again. Her eyes had danced with unself-conscious gaiety. Not since their first meetings had he seen her look so well.

He went back to his own hotel and waited, drinking the night away, his elbows on the table, his thoughts revolving endlessly. He was impatient to be with her, to discover for himself if she had forgotten him.

But on the next day when he arrived at the house, he was told that the family were all out. They would not be back until next day. Where had they gone, he demanded. And was told that they were visiting relatives.

"And the young Englishwoman?"

The footman's brows rose. "The English lady was with them," he was told icily.

He returned to his hotel and fell heavily asleep. It was early next morning when he awoke. He washed, shaved and dressed carefully, then went out to call on various old friends. He had revised his entire plan of campaign during the night.

He made no more visits to the house at which Sabine was staying. Instead, he accepted warm invitations from his friends to parties, balls, masques, and he began to lead a lively life.

His calculations were accurate. Within four days, he was a guest at a masked ball at which Sabine was to be present. He had discreetly discovered as much from his friends, who were quite amused by this turn of events. From them, too, he discovered that Sabine was currently the toast of Paris. The beautiful widow, so fair and so sweet-tempered, had captured the young men of the town, particularly since she was known to be a very wealthy widow.

His friends assumed that Falcon was discreetly investigating his young cousin-in-law, and tacitly assumed, too, that the rumors of her possible betrothal to her present host were well founded.

He lounged in a corner, watching the new arrivals, and saw her as soon as she entered. She was wearing a very pale pink-striped gown, her face masked with black velvet, a black fan dangling from her fingers. Falcon was glad to see her out of mourning. It was, of course, more than a year since Roger's death by now.

He watched her dancing with various men, eyeing her handsome host with great displeasure when he observed how closely the young man attended her. At last, with a very pretty young lady on his arm, he sauntered close enough for her to hear him, and, raising his voice, spoke in English about the weather and the sad crush in the room.

In one of the gold-framed mirrors which hung on the walls, he watched her and saw her stiffen and turn quickly, looking about. She saw him, and her lips parted in a quick breath. For a moment she stared hard, then she turned away again.

Satisfied, Falcon sauntered away. He danced every one of the dances, several times with the same girl, but all his attention was fixed on Sabine. And he was rewarded with the knowledge that she was as aware of his presence as he was of hers. Her eyes continually turned towards him, and her spirits seemed suddenly less cheerful.

Towards the end of the evening, he contrived to be near her as a dance was struck up and, without a word, seized her waist and whirled her away. She seemed struck dumb for a moment.

"You do not object to my unconventional behavior, ma'mselle?" he asked softly, holding her waist with a firm grip. "I have been watching you, and I never saw such a lovely mouth in my life. I just had to dance with you once."

Her mouth opened, then closed. She seemed suddenly very pale.

Whispering into her ear, he said, "Pink suits you, I am sure you know. You look like the inside of a shell. Like a rosebud. My heart beats faster whenever I look at you."

Still she did not speak, but he observed the flash of anger in her eyes and the tightening of her pink mouth, and he smiled.

"Why do you not speak, my angel? Those pretty lips were made to be kissed. If I had the courage, I would venture my life to snatch a kiss, but you have so many admirers, I am afraid I would be cut down like a dog in a second if I dared."

They were near the entrance to the dimly lit terrace, and he whirled her through the door and stopped beside the stone balustrade, looking out over the dark Paris streets.

She pushed at his chest as he moved closer, her eyes biting angrily through her black velvet mask.

Falcon smiled lazily. "Sabine, my darling love, won't you at least speak to me?"

Her hand froze on his chest. She looked up, her eyes searching his face.

He peeled off his own mask and looked down. "Did you really think I should not know you? Even if you wore an iron mask?" He put out a hand and gently took her mask off.

She was smiling now, but there were small tears shining in her eyes.

Falcon bent his head, and she clung to him, her mouth hot and eager under his, her arms round his neck.

"My darling, my love," he whispered, "I have come for you."

And she let her head droop on to his shoulder without a word of protest.

OTHER FICTION
FROM
PLAYBOY PRESS

LOVE'S BRIGHT FLAME $1.95
SHEILA HOLLAND

Eleanor of Aquitane was the richest heiress in medieval Europe. A woman of charm, intellect and explosive passion, she married Louis, King of France, in a political match that was to prove a personal disaster. Desired by many, her power blazed a fiery path across the continent leaving no man unmoved. But it was to Henry, King of England, that she gave herself completely and forever.

SWEET JAEL $1.50
SARAH FARRANT

A beautiful penniless orphan, Jael was hired as social secretary and companion to the mistress of Pengrail Park. Soon she fell desperately in love with Ralph, the lord of the manor and quickly resolved to have him at any price. Step-by-devious-step she plotted and planned, using all her charm, youth and "innocence" in a scheme to diabolically murder Ralph's wife and son and thus to become the sole mistress of Pengrail Park. A Victorian thriller.

THE SCANDALOUS LADY $1.50
MAGGIE GLADSTONE

As one of the dazzling Lacebridge belles, Sara was expected to marry a man of wealth and position. Instead she scandalized all polite society by running away, to pursue her dream of stardom on the London stage. There she set out to prove her worth, never dreaming that she would capture the heart of Covent Garden's most handsome and sought-after leading man. The first in a series of four delightful regency romances introducing the Lacebridge ladies.

ORDER DIRECTLY FROM:
Playboy Press
P.O. Box 3585
Chicago, Illinois 60654

No. of Copies		Title	Price
_____	E16435	LOVE'S BRIGHT FLAME	$1.95
_____	C16432	SWEET JAEL	1.50
_____	C16473	THE SCANDALOUS LADY	1.50

Please enclose 25¢ for postage and handling if one book is
ordered; 50¢ if two or more, but less than $10 worth, are or-
dered. On orders of more than $10, Playboy Press will pay
postage and handling. No cash, CODs or stamps. Send check
or money order, or charge to your Playboy Club Credit Key
#_____.

Total amount enclosed: $_____

Name _____

Address _____

City _____ State _____ Zip _____